DEATH PULLS A
Stake Out

ELIZABETH GUIZZETTI

Second Edition Paperback ISBN-13: 978-1-950708-26-0

Second Edition: Ebook ISBN-13: 978-1-950708-27-7

Dedicated to the socially anxious folks who crave to fit in but know themselves enough to be proud of who they are.

Dear Readers:

MAKE NO MISTAKE; THIS IS A COZY MURDER mystery about vampires. There is no swearing on the page. It is probably the cleanest book I've ever written, but it is about vampires.

This is the Second Edition of *Death Pulls A Stake Out*. Not much has changed except a round of editing, more illustrations. However one of the major changes is the book is now written in the first person. The reason it was originally released in the third person is because *Immortal House* was. That was silly. In fact, all the early drafts were in the first person. So I changed that in order to finish up the series the way I wanted it.

In this foreword, I would like to give you a bit of history of *Death Pulls a Stake Out,* because its a spin-off. Norma Mae Rollins first appeared as a secondary character in *Immortal House.*

I did not expect the setting of a dark comedy novella about a vampire named Laurence who was trying to purchase a home in 2018 to explode into my consciousness, grab hold of my gray matter, and order me to write about it. Yet that is what happened when I created Seattle's vampire coven: The Paper Flower Consortium.

As it is said, nothing is certain, except death and taxes, the coven primarily offers identification, documentation, mortgages, legal advice and accounting services to the supernatural community. With this in mind, ideas burst into my brain. I had so many characters and back stories, but I didn't know what I was going to do with them. A question tormented me: *how do I organize all these ideas into stories that people actually want to read?*

Step 1: Remember the vision and finish *Immortal*

House.

Step 2: Write a completely different book or series about another vampire.

It may surprise you, dear reader, Norma was not the first character I explored for her own book. I originally wrote a skeleton draft for a book about Derrik and Pascaline. (Don't worry if you don't know who these people are yet, you will meet them on the following pages.) After all, they also were in *Immortal House,* and lived interesting lives. However, the seemingly fearless and quick-witted, lover of cinema, Norma was just too much fun not to have her own series. By her very nature, her character forced the universe to expand around her. Her scenes hinted of a life Laurence barely knew. And I thought: *If Norma had her own books it could be a series of mysteries!*

I never wrote a mystery before so I did some research and did the Three-Day-Novel Challenge and wrote a first draft story about Norma in 2018 solving a crime which reminded her of her relationship with her creator back in 1951. That story is never going to see the light of day--or if it does it needs to be heavily edited--but it helped cement the ideas I had about a vampire driving around in a van saving people of all species. For readers of *Immortal House* or other books in the *Paper Flower Consortium Universe*, please remember that book was written from another vampire's point of view. While the history is the same, but Norma's books are written from her point view and she does not see her early years as a vampire through the rose-colored glasses of nostalgia.

Immortal House hints at Norma's struggles, *Death Pulls a Stake Out* shares a more complete story of who she was as a human, who she is as a vampire, and the existence she leads.

I hope you enjoy Norma's first book.

-Elizabeth

July 27, 2019

Chapter 1

8:10 PM

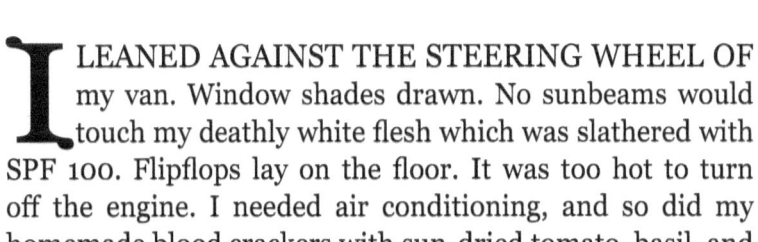

I LEANED AGAINST THE STEERING WHEEL OF my van. Window shades drawn. No sunbeams would touch my deathly white flesh which was slathered with SPF 100. Flipflops lay on the floor. It was too hot to turn off the engine. I needed air conditioning, and so did my homemade blood crackers with sun-dried tomato, basil, and goat cheese filling. The canapes were in a cooler, but it crept toward a hundred degrees out there.

Human movies always showed vampires rising at sunset and going to sleep at sunrise. Maybe that schedule worked in an equatorial region, but not in Seattle. The sun wouldn't set tonight until 8:56 pm. I assumed there were vampires — like the ones from movies—who were so wealthy, they didn't need a job, but I had never met a one-percenter. Even the most ancient vampires in my coven could not afford to keep themselves and their enthralled humans in modern comfort without employment. Sure, compound interest helped, but Seattle was an expensive city.

My friend and employee, Carlos Fisher Perez, lugged groceries up the stairs to an elderly werewolf's townhouse. A shade (sometimes also called a zombie or revenant) had a slow, uneven gait, but even as his body slowly decomposed, Carlos was gifted with unnatural strength.

It wasn't the most exciting job, but not all jobs were

exciting. While Norma's Cleaning Service was originally for vampires when hunting got a little messy, my company now ran all types of errands for the supernatural community. By hiring a shade, I was able to expand the hours and service list.

The client ultimately planned on getting a ramp installed but was waiting on insurance and approval from his HOA. The old werewolf could no longer control his turning. It was not safe for others if he left his house with a senior's group. Delivery people sensed a monster lived in the house and refused to climb the steps. Instead, they left packages on the sidewalk to be stolen before the old werewolf could collect them.

Once Carlos returned, he lifted the werewolf and his wheelchair and transported him securely into his home. He bounded down the stairs and scrambled into the van's passenger seat. He tugged at his shirt to signal: "Damn, it's hot" and tapped on the clock.

"Let's see if we get one more job."

Carlos shrugged and texted a single word: **buffet**, which echoed through my van's Bluetooth system in the phone's robotic voice.

I had promised Derrik Miller —my former guardian, mentor, and the vampire who made the vampire who created me — I would come home for the Sabbath Mass and Fellowship this week. However, that meant I was leaving money on the table. Something about sunshine made people stupid, especially when twilight was incapable of eliminating the day's heat. Still, Mass didn't start until eleven. Afterward, we'd spend the night with Derrik, his enthralled human, Hugo, and Hugo's elderly mother, Maria. Since the nights were so short, Carlos would take the van home, and I would spend the coming day with Derrik. Then, Carlos would pick me up tomorrow. There was no reason to hurry.

"Don't worry; we'll make it."

Carlos: **Hope they have that shrimp again.**

"The ones Marion made? Don't know, but Derrik made ceviche. He asked if there were anything you'd especially want in it."

Maria's recipe?

"Yep."

YUM.

Hmmm. Maybe Maria is the reason Derrik asked me to come home this week? "Hey, did I mention she's moving into a studio apartment down the hall from them once her lease is up?"

Carlos shook his head.

"There's an empty enthralled studio for rent. Wait. You don't think this is a trap to help her move, do you?"

If so, they better have beer.

Thinking I might be asked to do a favor for Maria and Hugo made me more willing to go, not less. I didn't mind spending time with the vampire family as long as something was going on. I always attended the annual meetings and important Sabbaths, such as initiations and weddings, but often skipped July when all everyone did was complain about the lousy sunshine. I was just happy I could bring Carlos, and everyone liked him well enough.

My phone rang.

Frightened, fast English spilled through the van's Bluetooth system from a haunting melancholy voice. Possibly male.

"I heard you help everyone. I didn't mean to do it. This woman won't stop taking my picture. She claims she loves mermen. I don't want to hurt her. I'm trying to help, but she won't stop touching me. What do I do?"

"One job," I mouthed and said, "First of all: who are you?"

"Samuel Poseidonson."

Poseidonchild, Poseidondottier, or Poseidonson were

a merperson's public name. Their private surnames were only used in their community.

"Where are you?"

"Golden Gardens."

I turned down Seneca until First Avenue and headed north. I glanced at the clock. "I'll be there in twenty minutes. She's still with you?"

"Yeah, I pulled her from the water. She's shivering ... and it's going to get dark. Probably pretty cold for a human. Wait. Can vampires cross moving water?"

Carlos made a grunting sound which was a mix of hiccups and laughter.

"As long as Ballard Bridge is down." I rolled my eyes at the old myth. "We assume her boat is wrecked."

"Yeah, but I didn't mean to do it. I'm not even a great singer."

The voices of merfolk were legend — even the poorest singers among them sang better than most vampires.

Slathering another layer of sunscreen over my face, I asked, "You're not in the sandy part?"

"No. We're hidden in the rocks."

"Good. See you soon."

At the next stoplight, I engaged the emergency brake and grabbed a floppy hat on the floor behind my seat. The light changed. I released the emergency brake, turned onto Denny, and followed 15th Avenue northwest toward Ballard.

WRAPPING A BEACH TOWEL AROUND MY arms to protect my undead skin from the sinking sun, I held a bottle of water and a basic first-aid kit and raced down the trail. The burning orb was still above the horizon, but soon it would be twilight, and I would be safe until it rose again.

The woman shivered beside Samuel on the most

northern stretch of rocky beach. A sea lion sat beside them and barked at my approach. Pieces of the shattered hull of her rowboat lay on the rocks below.

Samuel's sleek, muscular body was covered in a beautiful iridescent shade of algae green to camouflage him when in the water, and his full chest of tattoos was spectacular. He was a half meter longer than an average adult vampire (or human) male was tall. Trying to protect the woman from the breeze off the water, he twisted his long, shimmering finned tail around her and sat with his back to the Sound.

The human was in her early thirties with sun-bleached reddish hair set in two messy braids for her day on the water. Her toned, tanned skin had a few patches of pink where she had been sunburned. She looked vaguely familiar, but I couldn't place where I had seen her before.

"I'm Norma Rollins."

The woman raised her hand and waved drunkenly. Her brown eyes swam.

"You're just a kid." With the expression of a befuddled puppy, Samuel cringed away from the painted fingernails running up his arm.

"Hi, Norma, I'm Ivy. He won't give me back my phone." She pouted and ran her hand on his arm again. This was not right. Perhaps, Ivy was one of the ladies who got too interested in the film *The Shape of Water* and the subsequent flood of merman porn.

"I'm older than I look," I answered Samuel.

Outwardly, I appeared to be a fourteen-year-old, but was reborn seventy years ago. While I could dress to look older when necessary, Seattle was a casual city. It was better to blend in. My jeans had a ripped knee where the denim thinned. My purple t-shirt had a cute zombie and read **I see Undead People**.

I sat beside them on a rock, still warm. I forced opened their minds in order to see their thoughts.

Most vampires couldn't read minds per se, as much as their predator prowess allowed them to sense the variations in their prey's emotional state and automatic bodily responses.

However, thanks to Derrik's natural gifts and his insistence on education, his descendants read all species' minds pretty well. When the coven found me, Derrik feared for my well-being due to my small stature and the scandal of my creation. As my telepathic and empathic training had been extensive, my gifts were considered impressive, even among my bloodline. I could also hypnotize, remove memories, and instill panic. I had to work on dominating people, because no one took my outer shell seriously.

Samuel was easy to read. He wanted to go home and forget all this happened. Ivy's head was spinning with excitement she found a merman, but she was also high. She was confused about where her boat was. Weirdly, she wanted to be in a movie? *Or people to like her movie?* Maybe Ivy was an actress. She certainly was fit and pretty.

As the sun's last rays fell under the horizon, I placed the beach towel around Ivy and looked deep into her eyes.

"What's your name again?" I asked, carefully establishing a mental connection.

"I- I- Ivy."

"How much did you drink, Ivy?"

"I didn't." She giggled.

"Smoke?"

"I only use edibles." Marijuana was legal in Washington State for recreational use.

"Did you have anything else to eat or drink?" I asked.

"Just crackers and water."

"How much sun did you get today?"

"I was out all day."

"Did you drive here?" Something wasn't right; I looked deeper into Ivy's eyes.

"No, took the rowboat from Blue Ridge."

No wonder Ivy had great arms. "Do you live in Blue Ridge, near the water?"

Ivy nodded.

"You're dehydrated. You may have heat exhaustion. You need to rest. You're so exhausted you believe you saw a merman, but you saw a sea lion. A sea lion pushed your boat ashore and even barked to get help. I came to help you. Remember." I opened the bottle of water and handed it to her. "It will sound crazy, but that's how you know it's true. Fresh water, drink."

Ivy took the bottle. She patted my leg. Her heartbeat echoed in my mind. She stretched her head back and gulped down the water. The pulse under her tanned throat enticed my hunger.

"Why would a sea lion help?" Samuel asked, momentarily breaking my connection with Ivy.

I reestablished the connection and answered them both: "You realize the sea lion may've thought you were something else and it acted from some strange instinct. Remember."

"Remember," Ivy repeated. "Sea lion."

"Sleep. You're tired."

Ivy lay her head on a nearby rock.

"Sleep," I said.

Ivy closed her eyes.

"Let me see that phone, Samuel."

I took down Ivy's address. I deleted several pictures of the merman. I went to permanently delete and removed them again with the hope there weren't any other backups.

I tapped on the connected social media apps on Ivy's phone. I checked Facebook, which apparently Ivy rarely used. I checked Twitter, which fortunately Ivy primarily used for work; she had not posted or tweeted. On Instagram, I deleted a post that showed the outline of a merman singing and replaced it with a photo of a sea lion singing. I erased a video, which caught the haunting music. I kept the images of the "shipwreck" as there were a few of Ivy's followers questioning her whereabouts.

I whispered in Ivy's ear, "Who saved you?"

"A sea lion," Ivy whispered, still half in a trance. "But why does the sea lion wear tattoos?"

"It isn't tattooed; its blond hair darkens as it matures. Perhaps that's why it was interested in your boat. It was playing," I said, "You lost your phone in the water. You were posting to Instagram and lost it."

"I lost my phone in the water," Ivy replied. "What are you? Don't I know you from somewhere?"

I could figure out how we knew each other later. Right now it wasn't important. "Just a teenager. I spotted your crash from the beach and went to get help."

"Help from the beach," Ivy repeated. Her head fell backward. I cradled her head and rested it upon the ground. She snored lightly.

"So that's it?" Samuel asked.

"Yeah. Three hundred dollars, please."

"I don't have it on me. I mean I just went out."

I handed him my card. "I take credit, debit, or you can pay me online."

Samuel rose on his tail to tower above me. "What does a kid like you need three hundred dollars for anyway?"

Since I opened my business six decades ago, new customers have always questioned my need for money.

"I have a mortgage and a car payment like anybody. Living offshore, you have no idea how high Seattle property taxes are," I told him.

"There's plenty of Poseidonsons." He edged toward the water.

Carlos walked down from the sidewalk. His feet shuffled in the sand. He lifted his phone and took a photograph.

Samuel turned, his fangs bared, long claws expanded

from his webbed fingers as he flexed. He was taller than Carlos, but when Carlos set his dead, vacant stare upon anyone, they were suddenly aware of the lean, muscular Latino whose shoulders appeared to be hewn from solid oak. Of course, there was also all the flesh-eating stereotypes associated with the walking undead.

"True, but only one has your specific arrangement of tattoos," I said. "I'm pretty sure the next Poseidonson who needs my help wouldn't be all that forgiving to you when he discovers why I won't work for him. My fees are clearly posted on my website and flyers. If you need installments, say so. We can set something up."

Samuel laughed nervously as Carlos grew closer. I knew he'd pay. Clients always paid.

"I should've drowned her," he growled.

I knew he didn't mean it. Merfolk didn't look kindly on merfolk who went around drowning less capable swimmers such as humans. Not only was this a terrible stereotype about their species, but it also brought curious humans closer to discovering their underwater cities.

"Online is okay?" Samuel said, "Could we split it over three months? $100 tonight, $100 on the last of the month. The $100 two weeks later on my payday."

"That'll be fine." I snapped Ivy's phone in half.

"Thanks for your help. I shouldn't have to change my activities for humanity. They don't hide. Why should we be forced to? If anybody should pay, it's Ivy."

"I agree, but I don't make the rules." I put my hands on my hips. "You called me. I came to help. If I can get something from her, I'll give you the exact amount as a discount. Speaking of humanity, I need to get Ivy home."

"What are you going to do with her?" Samuel asked.

"Put her in a cab."

"Oh, I thought you ate them." He sounded disappointed.

"Sometimes I do, but if I ate her, I'd be higher than a

kite and unable to drive around Seattle saving people from themselves." I spoke in half-truths to uphold my vampire street cred. "And you don't want to see a shade high. They go all *Dawn of the Dead* on you."

Carlos gently woke Ivy and lifted her to her feet.

"Oh, you're a brute!" Ivy giggled and kissed him.

The former luchador turned his head, so her lips grazed only his cheek.

It bothered him how people judged and interacted with us based on our outer-shells. He despised people who harassed us.

Many saw only the fourteen-year-old me, but some humans, werewolves and vampires saw a "tough looking Mexican dude" and thought nothing of picking fights with him or asking if he was a day laborer. Straight women and gay men sometimes made sexual advances. People didn't see the guy who loved his cats and used his commute time on the Sounder from Tacoma to Seattle to indulge in reading or watching his favorite BookTubers.

A lesser shade might have ripped open Ivy's throat and eaten her alive, but Carlos didn't do drugs.

Plus, he wanted to save room for the buffet.

Chapter 2

10:12 PM

WET AND SMELLING VAGUELY OF THE shore, I used a burner phone to call a cab. I ensured the driver knew Ivy's address, paid $40 in cash — probably more than double the fare -- and watched as the cab started northward.

In the van, Carlos tapped the clock. **10:12**

Crap. By the time we crossed Seattle to Georgetown, showered and changed our clothing, we would be late for the Sabbath. Still, we would easily make the Fellowship.

Forty-three minutes later, we entered the garage of the unassuming brick building with just enough art deco embellishment to proclaim the era of its construction. I parked in one of my two parking spaces. I pulled the canapes from the cooler. The filling had held up perfectly.

Carlos and I slipped through a side door which took us up a ramp to the first level where the Consortium vampires kept their offices. All American vampire coven were nonprofit entities which acted as a mix of an extended family unit, business, and condominium association. The Paper Flower Consortium was a mid-sized, mixed use, seven-story tower with condo apartments on the upper floors and businesses on the ground level. Member vampires and their enthralled humans worked together so the coven could exist in security and agreeable comfort. Most also called it home. Though I resided on Capitol Hill, I owned a commercial space with two parking spots and kept my headquarters there. Derrik had been disappointed when I didn't buy a condo in the building after college.

I loved my office. My desk, bookcase and file cabinet were waxed maple, which reminded me of the sun. My chocolate-brown, upholstered leather desk chair and sofa matched. Landscapes painted by local artists lined sky-blue walls.

I scribbled down: $100 payments 3x online. Hopefully, Samuel would be prompt in his payment. It annoyed Jakub and his team of accountants when my bookkeeping was out of whack due to partial payments.

I hurried into my office's private bathroom and turned on the water to my shower. It spurted from the old plumbing, cold as it always did. Waiting for the water to warm, I picked from my old Sabbath dresses in the closet covered in a dress bag with lemon sachet. I selected the vintage 1950's gray puffy skirt embellished with a single white rose and a black blouse with embroidered white roses on my chest. I laid it across my desk. Before Saturday nights became the busiest night for Norma's Cleaning Service, I dressed for every Sabbath as Derrik and the other vampires expected.

After my shower, I pulled up my hair and put on a little mascara and lipstick, but didn't bother with the matching sweater or tights. Even with the lower body temperature of vampires, the Fellowship Halls would be sweltering with heat from the humans. The air conditioning system was thirty-three years old, several years past the suggested replacement on the association's reserve study. After his shower, Carlos changed from his *Norma's Cleaning Service* tee to a button-down silk shirt, but he didn't wear a jacket either.

I noticed how he cracked his knuckles and rubbed the soreness in his hands. I hoped rigor mortis wasn't starting. The drugs in his system had stopped the stages of death, but the werewolf who accidentally changed him wasn't sure how many months or years it would be until Carlos met his final end. It was two years and counting. I did not want our friendship to ever end.

Derrik would be annoyed we weren't fully dressed. I slipped my engraved bleeding knife into my hidden skirt pocket, beside my phone. I didn't know if I needed it, but if I fed, it would please him if I had it – like a real vampire.

I thought of several other things I'd rather do with Derrik than church and a vampire fellowship. We could go to a movie and discuss the film like we did when I was young. Or one of Seattle's many museums. Or even up to the Space Needle to see the city lights and the newly-built rotating glass floor. It was touristy, but King County residents got a pretty good discount.

From the office, Carlos and I walked through an underground passageway to the heart of the Consortium. The oldest structure, the timber-framed barn had been renovated into a chapel and public meeting room after the consortium's other buildings were built.

I recognized the melody for *Dieu a Cree le Sang (God Created Blood)* as I placed the crostini on the buffet table and marked the blood-soaked basil crackers for vampires and regular for everyone else. I glanced at the large wooden clock on the wall and started the countdown to departure in my head. Twelve hours, maybe thirteen, at most. I didn't say it aloud and wouldn't even think it once inside the temple, because I didn't want Derrik to hear any urgency to get to my real home.

We took a seat in the rear pew. Since Carlos wasn't a vampire or religious, he wrote things which he would likely say through the night on color-coded cards. I knew the steps of the rite out of memory, but as I wasn't religious, I mused how outside this building was one of the most casually-dressed American cities in shorts and t-shirts. Inside, male vampires wore three-piece summer weight suits; females wore long black gowns of various eras and regions. Gender fluid and younger vampires were more capricious in their ensembles, but they still dressed for the Sabbath in fine fabrics and lace.

In the front row, Agata and Jakub sat with the leaders from the Bellevue coven. The two covens had long been allies with many friends from both groups intermixing and at times, intermarrying. Agata, the eldest vampire of the Paper Flower Consortium, was a wise woman both in the ancient and current meaning of the words. Hitome and Kanae, the eldest of their coven, had also been midwives in Japan and the women bonded over shared experiences.

The other visiting vampires from Bellevue along with their enthralled humans, Agata, and Jakub's enthralled humans filled the second row.

In the third row sat Agata's daughters and Jakub's sons and their enthralled.

Derrik's glossy blond waves were easy to spot beside Hugo and Maria in his traditional seat on the left side. Pascaline lay in her glass coffin on a gurney. She was in torpor — the long sleep which vampires often need after a few centuries of undeath. *Where was her enthralled human, Ethan Tupper?* He usually sat with the coffin.

Loretta and Charles sat to Derrik's right with their enthralled. Loretta and Charles fell in love and married as Agata and Jakub had planned for them. Pascaline and Derrik married with noble intentions and felt great fondness for each other, but they were not in love. The offspring of Loretta, Charles, Pascaline, and Derrik filled the pews behind them.

A quick movement in a pew a few rows ahead of me caught my attention. Instead of his standard seat, Ethan sat beside a younger man with the same sandy hair. The younger man kept slipping his phone in and out of his gray tweed jacket's pocket. Was he trying to dress appropriately and blend with the grays and blacks of the coven? He must be sweating buckets under the winter weight jacket. Maybe he was a possible initiate.

Perhaps, that's why Derrik asked me to come! Maybe Derrik wants another offspring.

Everyone stood for the final hymn. The young man fidgeted with his phone again. Ethan hissed something, but I couldn't make out the words over the music.

Twenty-seven coven vampires, the visiting vampires, their assorted thralls, and hired domestic staff filed out of the temple into the public parlor.

The vampires moved languidly. They stood too still. The older they got, the less they needed to fidget or even blink. The humans' swift heartbeats sounded like rabbits awaiting slaughter. Except there was no killing in the coven. It was all pretend danger.

Medieval Romanian folk music filled the parlor. After the Romanian music, the band would play songs from 16th Century Japan to honor the visiting leaders of the Bellevue coven as it was proximately the 16th century when they braved the oceans. The music would move forward through the centuries and several countries until it became decidedly American and modern throughout the night.

Existence in the coven was a strange mixing of times as treasured moments were replayed weekly. In the long centuries which they existed, vampires were often wistful for the simplicity of the time they were born - even though their lives before they were reborn were not easy ones. The weekly nostalgia made me cringe and regret my vintage skirt and blouse. I never wanted to be stuck in the 1940s or '50s.

I sought friendly faces. Someone jostled me from behind. Marion Betsy Crabtree, a vampire not even fifty years since her rebirth snarled, "What's the Shame doing here?" under her breath as she went by with her lover from the Bellevue coven on her arm.

"Hi, Marion, Roger," I tried. Carlos grunted and bowed

his head.

"Good evening," Marion said in her vampire way as if the world hadn't turned from formality in the years she was born.

"Your hair looks pretty," I said.

"Thank you." Before she was changed, Marion's hair had been highlighted with various shades of blonde transforming her natural brown color. Her hairstylist had been excellent at his craft. I sometimes wondered if her hairstylist would be delighted to know his work would last forever.

Roger smirked and muttered: "Your thrall smells of death."

Ignoring the rudeness, I smiled. "Really? He's my friend, not my thrall. Have you met? This is Carlos Fisher Perez."

Carlos handed Marion a card which read: Hello, Marion, I enjoy your shrimp. And handed Roger a card which read: The pleasure is mine.

Marion laughed. She had a great smile and the infectious laugh of a happy woman, but she never indicated those traits to me. The coven's chief of security, Marion zealously believed in and followed the law. Even though I existed before she was reborn, she hated seeing the undead reminder that a coven brother of The Paper Flower Consortium had broken regulations.

Pascaline's offspring, Alice, who moved to Bellevue to work with new technologies and marry an ancient vampire, meandered up to Marion with a human on her arm. Roger introduced the human to the vampires. He ignored Carlos.

Alice kissed my cheek and said I looked well.

I returned the greeting and introduced Carlos.

Alice smiled frostily. "When will you be introducing your family to a thrall? You know Derrik and Pascaline only want what's best for you."

"But then I suppose you can't, can you?" Marion added.

Pushing frustration into my stomach, I finished the conversation as politely as I could.

Carlos passed me a card. I don't care about vampire snottiness. I'm here for the free meal and to hang with your real family.

Geez, how did he know to have that card ready?

He growled with a laugh in his throat and handed me the next card. Dude, this place is always 50 shades of strange.

Feeling lighter and less alone, I laughed and handed the cards back.

Jakub took the blood from his newest thrall, Summer Dahlgard, who worked for the coven's IT department. Jakub was thirty-eight when Agata changed him. In the modern age, he looked to be in his mid-forties. His pale skin around his eyes bore a spiderweb of lines. His high forehead gave him a distinguished look, especially with his dark Shakespearean hair which fell over his shoulders and his long brown beard touched with silver. His suit was somewhat close to current, but under it, an older style shirt, trimmed with lace.

I would say hi to them later.

Agata rushed to me with her thrall, Kuma Michaels. Her medieval long brown braids were bound into a thick bun at the base of her neck. Rubies and diamonds were set about her throat. Her black silk and lace gown trailed across the wood floor. Attacked long before consent laws changed the vampire existence, Agata was transformed early in her third decade and walked with timeless beauty, but her smoky eyes didn't blink enough to pass as human. She embraced me in her silk-clad arms and kissed my cheeks.

I never doubted Agata's devotion to my wellbeing, even if the ancients had no idea how to care for a vampire changed outside the program. "How are you, dear heart? Have you fed tonight?"

"No, Bunică." (Romanian for Grandma.)

"Carlos, dear, I am so pleased you joined us again. I

ensured there were plenty of vegetables, red meat, and fresh fish on the buffet for you," Agata said. "And Kuma agreed to satiate you, Norma."

Cow's blood would have satisfied, but no doubt with company around, Agata wanted the coven's little abnormality to appear as normal as possible.

Carlos inclined his head in thanks and headed off to find the table.

Agata patted my hand as she and Kuma led me away. "You ought to let me know when you are coming, so we can always have someone ready for you. Or take your own thralls; you are certainly old enough. Nothing against Carlos, but he cannot feed you."

"That's gross, Bunică. We're friends."

"It is not gross, dear. It is how humans and vampires coexist safely," she said. Kuma agreed.

"And I'm his boss. It would be exploitive of me to use him in that way."

"Oh, Norma Mae, modern ethics will be the final death of me. Next, you will tell me our thralls are ill-used."

International laws forbid compelling an unwilling soul into thralldom, but I figured anyone who wanted to be a thrall for a vampire who looked forever-fourteen was a creep. Sometimes when bitter loneliness crept in my heart, I hunted such fiends and threw their bodies to the sea serpents. Since I wasn't a creep, unlike some fictional vampires, I didn't spend eternity hanging around high schools. I wouldn't enthrall someone who was the age I had been when I turned. Even if they were willing, they couldn't consent.

Agata and Kuma led me to a nearby burgundy velvet settee. The couches were as vibrant as they had been the day they were manufactured as the sun never touched these inner rooms. The vampires in their black and gray clothing looked striking against them, but the couches were chosen due to their ability to hide stray drops of blood.

I sat beside him; he held out his wrist. "It's been too long, Norma."

Kuma's eyes were an enchanting shade of hazel. The handsome man of mixed Korean and Japanese descent looked positively delicious in the black linen trousers and silk shirt he wore.

My previous hunger rose in the back of my throat. "You sure? You don't have to."

His smile became tight. He knew he did not *have* to. Our Home/Commercial Association owner declarations forbid vampires touching each other's thralls without permission. Thralls set the level of touch and bloodletting. His relationship with Agata was openly polyamorous. He often shared his blood with me or vampires visiting from outside the coven.

"I offered as soon as Derrik told us you were coming. Don't fear for me, your grandmother fed on Bernie tonight. Take as much as you need. Your pallor isn't good. Derrik's right. You're always working too hard."

I sliced open his brown wrist with my bleeding blade and sucked the wound. Sweet, salty iron rushed into my system. I felt stronger, more alive, warmer.

I ignored his body's enjoyment of bloodletting so as not to embarrass him. It wasn't about me, but the act of giving blood he enjoyed. When finished, I pretended not to see the vampires who watched me. I thanked him and gently bandaged his wrist. "Do you need a juice or coffee?"

"If it's not too much trouble, would you make me an Americano? I always get so tired when it's stuffy like this," Kuma said.

"Sure, I'll be right back. You want it hot?"

"Yeah."

"No problem."

Agata's oldest thrall, Bernie Golden glared. On his side, he and Agata had a monogamous relationship. He hated when I fed on Agata's thralls. I figured it didn't matter what Bernie thought since Agata and Kuma loved feeding me. I would never ask Bernie to do so.

I moved through the crowd to the espresso maker where I found Derrik creating the perfect latte for his thrall, Hugo Ramirez.

"Hello," I said over the sound of the espresso maker.

"How lovely you look." Hugo kissed my cheek.

More silver than black hair covered his head, and his brown face had matured into rugged lines as he edged toward sixty. He sported a summer weight linen suit, a shirt, and a tie in the rich blue of twilight.

Derrik's golden hair was set with tight finger waves, and his mustache was impeccably waxed. Though he would never use the term, he spent a lot of time manscaping. He appeared eternally twenty-seven, but between Derrik and Hugo, it was a toss-up who was more of a curmudgeon. They lived in a well-appointed two-bedroom Consortium apartment with a den, but I could easily imagine both shouting, "Get off my lawn!" if they'd had one.

A lawyer specializing in supernatural immigration and commercial law, Derrik seldom left the Paper Flower Consortium before midnight, six nights a week; on Sabbath didn't leave it all. Like me, he worked for the supernatural community at large; unlike me, he kept strict business hours. He never understood why I didn't. As if people reserved their stupidity for Monday through Fridays. Besides, with all the people I met on the job, I funneled him and the other businesses clients. He should be happy.

Derrik handed Hugo a latte. In the milk he had created a tulip as well as any barista in Seattle.

"Gracias," Hugo said.

Derrik embraced me and used the closeness to whisper: "I'm glad to see you aren't neglecting your family for another Sabbath." He worked hard to disguise his Cockney accent in the former century with the transatlantic accent of the radio age, but it became more prominent when he was annoyed. I wondered what random thought he had picked up.

Carlos ambled over with a plate of vegetables, ceviche, and a skewer of spiced grilled shrimp. Marion might not be the friendliest vampire, but she did know how to cook shrimp.

He held out a card which read: Hello Derrik and Hugo, thank you for inviting me.

Derrik bowed. "It's my honor to welcome you into my home. I am your servant, Sir."

Crap, if Derrik's falling back into Victorian salutations, he's really upset.

On another card: Your ceviche is wonderful. Norma told me you were making it.

"It's Maria's recipe."

"Where is Maria? I thought I saw her at the service," I asked.

"Napping before we go upstairs," Hugo said. "The shift to nighttime living will be a challenge."

"I'm glad she'll be coming to dinner," I said.

"Want anything?" Derrik asked Carlos who shook his head. "Norma?"

"An Americano for Kuma."

"Agata and Kuma fed you?"

The soft "ah" sounds grew long as his old accent surfaced even more. He was pissed. He turned on the coffee grinder and measured a double shot of espresso.

"Before I made it across the room. She was trying to make me appear normal with Bellevue watching."

"She only wants what's best for you."

I had heard that my whole undeath. Everyone wanted what's best for me as if I were still too young to know what was best for myself.

Derrik carefully pulled the shot. His blue eyes never left the espresso which pooled in the shot glasses. He flicked on the hot water and filled the demitasse cup. Kuma took it black. He handed it to me.

"Thanks. I'll be right back."

I plated a tiny cake and a crostini. I carefully brought the treats through the crowd to Kuma. "Just in case, you got hungry."

"You're always such a thoughtful spirit," he said. "Derrik's been pacing the floor for your arrival."

"I know. He made your Americano."

"Wonderful. He's the best barista among you. Thank him."

"I will." I thanked him again and returned to where Derrik and Hugo had pushed chairs together.

Derrik turned a cup of iced blood in his hand. He did not bloodlet publicly either in or outside the coven. Even when I existed in his home, I never saw him bleed his enthralled human, though I once walked in on him and Pascaline sharing a vampire's kiss. (Pascaline broke away and suggested I might enjoy listening to the radio or reading before the two of them locked themselves in his suite for an hour.)

"It makes us happy to know you are safe under the coven's roof." Hugo had been with Derrik for only thirty years. He did not have a hand in getting me past adolescence. I guessed he was tired of hearing Derrik's complaints about an ungrateful offspring who never visited.

"Come see me," I replied as I always did.

"You know what a hassle it is to find parking in your neighborhood?"

It was not a question. The Paper Flower Consortium had ample underground parking. My condo building in Capitol Hill did not.

"Or have lunch with me when I take office hours. We don't have just to see each other at the Fellowships."

I anticipated Derrik's habitual complaints, but he

surprised me by asking, "When was the last time you saw Ryan?"

Ryan Jones was Derrik's second offspring; my progenitor, Bill Caruso, was his first. A Doctor of Marine Biology, Ryan Jones was changed in 1985 at the age of thirty-six. If he were human, he'd be in his late sixties. I liked Ryan well enough, because Derrik loved him, but I wasn't friendly with Ryan or his lovers.

"Last time I was at the Fellowship," I replied. "Seven weeks ago?"

"Ryan's at Alki again. You work too much; he works too little," Derrik said. "Normally he, at least, comes to the Sabbath."

I didn't need mental gifts to see he was worried. Usually, Derrik considered it rude to discuss another vampire's habits.

"So you don't want another offspring?" I asked.

"Why would you think that? I have two who struggle; the last thing I need is another."

Choosing the most common issue for a vampire his age, I asked quietly, "Ryan is struggling? Did his mother pass away?"

"About ten years ago."

"He isn't behind in his HOA dues, is he?"

Derrik stiffened. He didn't like it when we spoke directly about money.

"Is he working?"

He didn't answer; he only stirred a spoonful of honey into his cup of blood. I understood Derrik's concern. Generally, when their birth families or first mortal beloved died, or they tired of their first vocations, eternity loomed over young vampires. It certainly had for Bill.

"How much is he behind?" I asked.

"Just..." Derrik said.

Hugo interrupted him. "He drained his savings. He's

drinking from the blood pantry."

"Has anything happened?" I asked.

"Irene left," Hugo said.

Irene was Ryan's enthralled human — I vaguely remembered that they tended to quarrel so I almost never saw her. "What were the circumstances?"

"She got tired of slinking around the coven in her underwear. She wanted a real life before it was too late."

Was that regret in Hugo's voice? It was hard to imagine Hugo saying he didn't have a real life. Derrik was generous to a fault and gave his enthralled humans anything they wanted. Hugo kept his job as a supermarket shift supervisor because he liked to step away from the all-encompassing needs of the coven and enjoyed the social aspects including a fantasy football league, not because he needed to work.

I didn't answer, because, across the parlor, Bernie screamed, "Lady Agata!"

Though Derrik neared the age where he could crush a human skull with his bare hands, Hugo drew a protective arm around him. Ready to take my lead, Carlos went to situation mode and stepped in front of both men.

Across the room, Agata pulled the vampire, Bai Xiao, off Pascaline's enthralled human, Ethan Tupper, who bled profusely. The bite mark on his cheek and scratches on his neck were not deep, but precious, sweet blood leaked from the man's face.

"No doubt, that'll levy a fine," Derrik muttered.

Only thirty-years younger than Derrik, Xiao was the oldest of the coven's second-generation vampires. After escaping rioters during the Chinese expulsion in Seattle, Charles and Loretta found him hiding in the nearby forest. Vampires loved beautiful people. Xiao was striking in his fury. His slim build was covered in a black summer-weight suit; his glossy straight black hair looked flawless and slick with pomade. He must have been exceptionally lovely in his vulnerability. Loretta wouldn't have been able to leave him to his fate. She never could, which is why she had over a dozen offspring. And Charles had ten of his own.

"Unless someone's messing around," Hugo said.

My eyes tracked the young human in his early twenties who had been with Ethan dashing from the parlor. He held a cell phone in his hands.

He looked yummy. I briefly wondered how he would taste, but I didn't know if he had signed a thrall agreement with another vampire.

Xiao broke away from Agata and punched Ethan.

"Stop!" Xiao's thrall, Fern, tried to pull him away from Ethan. He shoved her away. She cried as she hit the wall and recoiled against it.

I gasped. I rarely witnessed vampires behave in such a manner. It was against our Homeowner Association Rules to harm an enthralled human. The other vampires backed away from the violence.

To hell with tradition.

Derrik must have heard my thought. His fingertips grasped onto my arm, but I was too fast.

"I'm stopping this before someone meets their final death." Knowing it was utterly stupid, I moved toward the violence.

Red wine, blood, and shattered glass were spilled across the dark tile. I quickened my pace. "Xiao, what are you doing?"

Xiao turned. His eyes flashed red but softened back to gray when he glared into my face. The snarl tempered into an annoyed frown. "What do you want?"

"I think ... ?" I gestured at Fern.

Black steaks of mascara rolled down her pink cheeks and snot ran past her chin. Her dark curls were messily spilling from a swirling golden headband which matched the lace trim on her loose off-the-shoulder black crepe Sabbath dress. The blood in Fern's rapidly swelling shoulder seemed to localize around the inflammation. I wanted to sink my fangs in.

Xiao's eyes focused on his injured thrall. "Oh..."

"That bruise looks like it might be bad. Are you okay, Fern?"

"I'm okay, Norma. Thanks for being concerned, but I'm okay." Her voice was shaky, but she rose to her feet, still hanging onto the wall.

Xiao put his arm around her. She shook him off.

"I'm okay. Just startled. Please, get me a drink."

"I'm sorry, I didn't see you. I'm sorry," Xiao repeated several times. "Do you need a doctor? I'm sorry. I only saw Agata and Jakub. I didn't know you were there."

Whether it was carelessness or not, I didn't like what Xiao had done, but Fern had not requested assistance. If she had, Xiao might have faced coven justice. (In this case, most likely a fine.) However, as an enthralled human, Fern had a job within the coven and full medical, dental and vision. She might not wish to threaten her lifestyle by complaining about an accident.

However, the violence was not over. Bernie stood over Ethan screaming about tradition. Ethan punched Bernie.

Bernie fell back into a couch. "I ought to kill you," he shouted.

I jumped in front of Ethan before he could strike again. "What are you doing?"

"This is between humans, Miss Norma Mae, stay back," Ethan said in his low Southern drawl.

Trying to think of how to stop the fight, I said the first thing that came to mind, "I'd like to talk to Pascaline."

His eyes fell upon my face. "She won't hear you."

"Please? Would you take me anyway? You're bleeding and you ought to get cleaned up."

He touched his face and stared at the blood in his

hands. "All right." He threw one more glare at Bernie and took my arm.

As we passed my family's party, I said, "I'm gonna see Pascaline. Carlos, will you be okay? Anyone want to come?"

Carlos held out a card. *Anyone want to play Apples to Apples? I have it in the van.* He was good at finding things to do.

"We'll be fine," Derrik said.

July 28, 2019

Chapter 3

I AM

"WHAT WAS THAT ABOUT?" I ASKED AS we walked away from the whispers in the parlor.

"The world outside is changing. You try to live it. I fear Pascaline waking if you aren't here," Ethan said.

Once a musician, he traveled the world, settling in Seattle after meeting Pascaline. Now he looked like part of an aging nostalgia hair band. Ethan's golden locks had grown long and straggly. Untamed scruff and broken capillaries marred his complexion. He wasn't into taking care of himself anymore.

"I'm not leaving Seattle," I said.

"You ought to visit more often. Vampires are slow to change, but the coven's changing — and not all for the better."

"What do you mean?"

"Back in my and Bernie's day, a thrall gave themselves to one vampire. If they left that vampire, they left the coven, not flitted around under the vampire's nose."

"Is this because I drank from Kuma? I had both Agata's and Kuma's permission. Just as you and Pascaline allowed me to drink from you on occasion."

He looked down at me. "You're what you are, but grown men and women shouldn't be doing what they are doing. Pascaline will wake to vampires who act like jealous teenagers."

I still had no idea. That is not what I saw in the parlor. "Is Hugo doing something Derrik ought to know about?"

"Hugo has it so good he doesn't even see it. I'd give myself to Derrik in a heartbeat. Stable, good-looking, a bit boring maybe, but a bit boring looks pretty damn good when you get to my age. Ever watched how Derrik makes a cup of coffee? Scrambles an egg? Massages Hugo's neck? Hell, he's paying for Maria's apartment," Ethan said. "Pascaline sleeps, she can't do anything for me."

"She..." *pays your living expenses.* I stopped myself, not wanting to say the wrong thing. When Pascaline was awake, she worked as the coven liaison, organized charity benefits, and the initiates program which provided her with a salary. As long as he was enthralled to her, Ethan resided in her apartment and had a stipend for living expenses which she had set up before she went to sleep. But he didn't have access to her wealth or someone to care for him. Unlike Loretta and Charles, Derrik and Pascaline kept separate residences, so Ethan had that whole apartment to himself. Maybe he was lonely.

"Who was the young man with you?"

"What young man?" Ethan replied.

I immediately sensed the *evasion.* "He sat next to you in the temple and ran from the parlor holding his phone when Xiao and Bernie got mad. I thought he might be an initiate. He's pretty cute."

"Just some kid who came for the Sabbath. He got a taste of it. I doubt we'll see him again now he understands how private vampires are." Ethan gestured at the ceiling to let me know he spoke about the coven as a whole.

"I didn't see what happened," I pried.

"You know how kids take pictures of everything. He took a picture with his phone when Xiao had his mouth on Fern's neck and his hand up her skirt. Xiao overreacted. I tried to stop the violence before it got out of hand, but what does it matter? It's not like vampires can be caught on film."

"Vampires can't be caught on regular cameras, but clothing and cosmetics can. And what about Fern's privacy? I wouldn't like a picture of me like that floating around the Internet."

Ethan interrupted. "Fern and Xiao have a pretty public relationship."

"But she..." Trying to teach ancient vampires the current rules of consent were tricky enough, but Ethan had spent decades as an enthralled human.

"Fern wasn't facing the phone. It'll look like trick photography. Nothing more."

I sensed there was more, but Ethan was careful not to show too much emotion or thought. I detected the top layer of emotions: he was furious at the photo, Xiao, and both annoyed and glad I stepped in, but little else. If I forced his mind open, I would be breaking HOA bylaws. What happened at work, stayed at work, but in the coven, I followed the rules because I was too economical to risk a fine.

Ethan opened the door to the Sanctum. We walked down a long ramp to the thrall's efficiency apartment. While Pascaline's residence was on the second floor, by the clutter, he spent many waking hours there. A library of books and Blu-rays filled the bookshelf. In the kitchenette, I noticed two place settings in the sink.

"Coming to Derrik's?"

"Not tonight; I've other plans." Ethan opened the inner door. "I'll give you some privacy."

I descended a second ramp lit only by candles. At the bottom, I was in nearly complete darkness. I struggled to see even with my vampire's sight. The Sanctum was silent even from the hum of the building's mechanical systems to ensure a long soothing sleep. I had not lived long enough to need dormancy, but it was customary for a vampire after a century or two to need rest to maintain good health and it helped them "reset" their expectations of existence.

I moved toward the glass coffin in the center of the room. Not a speck of dust lay on the coffin kept clean by Ethan's polishing. In a loose flowing black nightgown, Pascaline lay in perfect repose with jars of earth around her. Her auburn curls offset her freckled ivory skin. In her alabaster hands, she held a black lace handkerchief.

"I wish you were up. I miss you so much," I said.

Pascaline did not answer or give any indication she knew I was in the room.

"The coven isn't the same without you. Even Derrik's not the same without you. He complains about everything. He's always annoyed with me.

"Ethan got into a fight with Xiao today. The coven's getting weirder or maybe I'm getting old. The only constant is young vampires acting like I should be ashamed of existing because I ruin their party."

Reborn of Agata, Pascaline and Loretta became vampires after the Sun King's soldiers murdered their family for being Protestant and used their manor as barracks. She, her infant daughter, Celeste, and Loretta, escaped. They grew thin as they ran through what little money and jewelry they had. Eventually, the ladies found Agata and Jakub. Pascaline and Loretta began to mend, but still so young, Celeste died from pneumonia, no doubt worsened by malnutrition. Once back to a healthy weight, Pascaline chose to be reborn, but Loretta had to wait six years for her twenty-second birthday. The sisters were equals in eternity.

I told Pascaline how the rise of phones with excellent video capacity would make my job harder and harder. I talked about how much I had come to rely on Carlos and wondered if I should take on a permanent employee after he was gone.

"Good evening, Norma," a male voice said from the door.

"Hi, Ryan!"

His angular features flickered in the candlelight and dark skin shone with the blue hue of undeath. His brown eyes were filled with deep sadness. He held a bucket of seawater. "Does our honored sister still sleep?"

"Yes."

"Aren't you coming to Derrik's?"

I looked at my phone. "Oops." Heat prickled my undead cheeks.

I kissed the glass over the sleeping vampire's brow. We were not even out the door when Ethan came into the Sanctum with Windex and washed the kiss away.

We left the Sanctum and passed the main parlor. Many had gone to their private apartments or circled off into their own parties. "I was there longer than I thought, but I miss Pascaline so much."

"Of course," Ryan said in the formal vampire way which meant I had no idea what he really thought. Vampires weren't supposed to miss each other. We were supposed to be cold-hearted predators, but if that were true why would we congregate in covens? Why call each other honored brother, sister, or sibling? Why proclaim the importance of bloodlines and why would have Derrik and Pascaline protected and mentored me?

We turned the corner of the long ramped windowless corridor and felt a slight pressure change. We came into the light of the garage. I observed Xiao open the passenger door of his car for Fern. Her wrist was in a splint, but she walked confidently again.

Ryan moved toward the car. "Derrik told me what happened. You okay?"

"Just a bad bruise on my shoulder and a sprained wrist because of how I fell," Fern said.

I was annoyed by her choice of words.

"Xiao, you ought to be more careful, especially as

you're learning to deal with the greater strength that comes with being over a century." Though Ryan spoke to Xiao, his eyes never left Fern's face.

"What would you know about that?" Xiao asked.

"Nothing. Only Derrik mentioned it was a frightening time for him."

"No doubt it was." Xiao said. "But, when Derrik turned a century, he had other issues, including an insane offspring who shamed the coven and raising a child who wasn't his responsibility. I was there; you were not."

"But I was," I said.

"No one asked you. You were not a member of the coven, but a lost and frightened child."

"But Derrik was afraid he'd hurt someone. Ryan's just ... trying to help." My words sounded weak in my ears, especially when I could sense Ryan's heart aching - the rush of wanting to embrace someone, kiss them. I assumed Fern.

Xiao might not be able to read minds, but he had eyes. He hissed, "You seem a bit too concerned about my enthalled's health, my honored brother."

"We're friends," Fern said. "Xiao, take me home. I'm still sore."

"Do you need me to carry you?" Xiao's focus shifted from Ryan to Fern. He put his arm around her. "I will. Maybe you shouldn't climb the stairs tonight, especially in heels. The doctor said those painkillers might make you dizzy."

"I'll be fine. It's only four flights."

"At least, lean on me."

Fern allowed Xiao to assist her. As they climbed the steps ahead of us, I noticed the inner heel of Xiao's black shoes were a brilliant shade of blue. *So cool.*

Once he was sure they were out of earshot, Ryan muttered, "Fern needs someone gentler."

I wasn't sure if I should answer or not. Seconds of silence went by. I changed the subject. "What're you collecting? Are you studying something for work?"

The bucket splashed over its edge as he missed a step. "What work is there for a vampire marine biologist? I've been making sea salt for some of the thralls ... and collected a few snails for my tank."

"Derrik and Hugo are worried. They said Irene left."

"She did."

"Don't get upset, but..."

"Whenever people say that, it pretty much means I will be upset."

"Derrik said you're a little behind in your dues," I whispered though no one was around.

Ryan lowered his voice. "Derrik talked about money?"

"Well, no. He talked about both of us missing Sabbaths. I guessed by his frowns. I can give you a loan if you need one."

"No, I'll catch up. I didn't realize how much I'd miss being a marine biologist."

"Why'd you stop?" I asked.

"I can't find work, get grants. My peers are retiring." Ryan smiled sadly. "Just need to figure out what my next job will be."

I frowned. I didn't understand why any vampire would want to be unemployed and dependent on the coven. *Maybe if I offered Ryan a job, Derrik would get off my back about the Sabbaths. I'd even be hanging out with another vampire which would please Agata.* "If you want something to tide you over, I could use a driver when Carlos and I are with clients. The work has been steady for sixty-years; I can't imagine it going away."

When we arrived at the second floor, Ryan let me into his apartment. Like most vampire dwellings, the walls were painted an oppressive gray, and the windows were covered with black, interior solid shutters.

"If it comes to needing any job, I might take you up on it. Even if the only reason you're offering is to make Derrik happy. Thank you. I just need a little time."

Like me, Ryan was blessed with Derrik's empathic gifts. I would have to be more careful. I tried to backtrack. "Lots of people get jobs because they have a connection."

"Don't lie when I can see you're lying. Want something?" He asked as he set his bucket in his sink.

"A glass of water, please. Talking to Pascaline was a one-sided conversation."

He poured me a tall glass of cold water and himself a shot of cow's blood from his fridge.

A single painting of abstract, vaguely African pattern in gray, red, and black hung over the fireplace. I appreciated art but didn't know much about African-American art. "Who painted that?"

"Some street artist on the waterfront. I bought it when I was an initiate. Now it holds the memory of one of my last days in the sun."

I smiled. "That's nice."

He went into his suite. I studied the titles on his bookshelf as the shower turned on. Most of the books were nonfiction about sea animals and climate change. I noted a few books by Poseidon's children. At his desk, he had a closed laptop. My fingers grazed over the computer. Too bad people didn't write on paper anymore. I couldn't peek at his laptop. It probably was password-protected.

The shower turned off. I scurried back to the bookcase.

Ryan came out of his room. He looked solidly good in his black shirt, red tie, and red suspenders. His black pinstripe suit was broken up by a red tie and pocket square. When he dressed, he tended to be tailored, not delicate. I fleetingly imagined if I had been twenty-five when I was changed.

"I've been wondering if I should say something, but stepping in between that fight was beyond stupid."

"What do..."

"As I told Xiao not ten minutes ago, Derrik told me

when he called. It got me thinking. Your body's growth froze at fourteen, was your brain able to finish developing? Maybe that's why you can't help being nosy."

"I didn't look at your laptop," I said quickly.

Ryan straightened his tie. "No, but you were thinking it. I remember being fourteen. I took thousands of risks because I thought I'd live forever."

"But we will exist forever," I replied.

"Not if you look at people's laptops and get between older vampires and their thralls." Ryan held the door for me.

"I could say the same about you. It's dangerous to get behind."

He gently took my arm. "Jakub won't foreclose on my condo. It's only drama in an adolescent brain."

As we walked down the hall to Derrik's apartment, I whispered, "But don't you worry about climate change?"

"Of course, but I don't understand why you're thinking about it."

"Georgetown is only 13 feet above sea level, what if the coven has to move?"

A deep laugh erupted from his mouth as he knocked on Derrik's door. "You're proving my hypothesis. If the seas rose tomorrow, I'd ask Jakub and Derrik for help, and they would help me. Jakub has given loans with terms over a century."

"Yeah, I guess." I laughed with him, but I didn't think it was funny. Right or wrong, the coven judged vampires who got behind on their home association dues. And when things got bad, they were the first to fall.

HUGO, MARIA, CARLOS, AND DERRIK WERE still playing *Apples to Apples* when we arrived. We all played a few more rounds. Then Ryan beat us soundly at *Scrabble* with all his science words until Derrik went to make a light supper at 5 AM.

43

We, vampires, had chicken salad mixed with blood and mayo on lettuce leaves. We had a large cup of iced cow's blood so we could stomach humanesque food. The others had a more familiar chicken salad and their drink of choice.

Pushing more on Carlos's plate, Maria asked if he wanted to go to the human Mass with them in the morning while Derrik and I slept.

He had a card which read: Must head home to feed the cats after this delicious meal but thank you.

Derrik was disappointed to hear Ryan only sent out three resumes all week. "You might take advantage of the coven's reeducation grant," Derrik suggested, "Return to the university if you're not sure of your path."

Ryan said he had to think about it.

The conversation got more awkward. Derrik and Ryan debated whether collecting snails for one's fish tank was considered work on the Sabbath. This somber exchange led into Derrik's complaining about how I worked on the Sabbath and missed the first two hymns.

I took the criticism without an eye roll. Derrik, Ryan, (and Pascaline when awake) regularly commented on my lack of religious conviction. Tonight, Maria agreed with them. Hugo said nothing.

Thankfully, Carlos asked for a drink.

Derrik returned to host mode, but he complained about how I existed in a regular condo in Capitol Hill instead of in the safety of the coven. "Seattle neighborhoods are filled with homeless humans. The werewolf population is growing with the human population. I have so many werewolf clients. Not to mention the witches and demons and fey. It isn't safe for vampires anymore."

Then things got really uncomfortable.

"I don't blame dear Carlos, who is kind and good-hearted, but it's dangerous to sleep with a shade. Who knows when rot eats his body? Have you collected his earth?" Derrik asked.

Carlos choked and scrawled his innocence on a spare card. I'd never sleep with Norma. I'm not the type of guy to seduce my boss. She isn't the type of woman to seduce her employee.

I appreciated he didn't mention my outer appearance.

Carlos scribbled: My body may be going to rot, but Norma gave me a living-wage job while it does. I can't wrestle anymore. I'm happy to enjoy my boss's company as much as I do. I appreciate how often her family invites me over, but we are not together.

"He lives with his cats in Tacoma," I added.

"So, he's not your boyfriend?" Maria asked.

"No. He works for the Cleaning Service. We're friends. Whatever gave you the idea we were together?"

"All the young people sleep with their friends nowadays. They call it 'friends with benefits'," Maria said with an old woman's confidence. "I've read about it in several advice columns."

I blushed.

Maria continued: "Out there on the Hill, you're still going to clubs every night? Taking blood from strangers?"

"Well, not every night," I said.

"That's why Derrik worries," Maria scolded. "Time to settle down."

"Agreed," Hugo said. "I've never met another vampire who carried earth from their mother's garden. Or from their former guardians' home. Not a one."

Vampires carried the earth of anyplace they called home. I couldn't be the only vampire in the whole world who had earth from my mother's garden. Just because the other vampires of the coven only had their lovers' dirt, didn't mean all vampires did. Hugo had to be wrong.

Chapter 4

10 AM

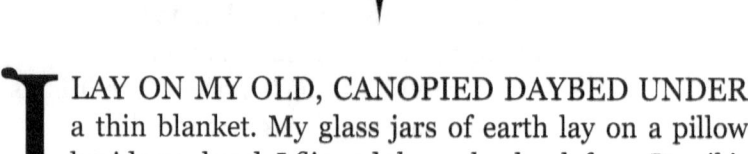

I LAY ON MY OLD, CANOPIED DAYBED UNDER a thin blanket. My glass jars of earth lay on a pillow beside my head. I flipped through a book from Derrik's bookshelf but spent more time staring at the curtains.

Like all vampires, I needed the sleep of the dead. That could only happen when I felt secure. Unable to sleep and stuck until Carlos returned, I wondered why I agreed to stay the day with Derrik. Though I loved him, I didn't belong in my old coffinroom — even with my old earth beside me.

I rolled to my side and stared at the empty fireplace flanked by two tall floral murals which my former tutor, Laurence, and I painted to brighten the never-ending gray. Derrik had filled the bookshelves with masses of his romance novels and highly detailed matchstick replicas of buildings, ships, and anything else which caught his fancy. There was a detailed half-finished Washington State Ferry on my old school desk and the closet was filled with his and Hugo's off-season clothing.

Otherwise, the guestroom looked like it had when it was called Norma's room. The oak coffin, inlaid with delicate roses, had been made for me. As beautiful as the coffin was, I never slept there. Eventually, Derrik bought the daybed but required the canopy of thick-layered curtains which would block any sun. After I moved out, the old furniture provided perfect accommodation for a visiting vampire and thrall.

I wondered if Derrik and the other vampires would ever accept me when a deep voice shouted a profanity. It sounded like it was just through a wall.

Bill.

I rolled off my daybed and crawled under it. Frightened tears sprang to my eyes and caused a lump in my throat. *Bill has come home. Derrik will be happy with him in a way he has never been with me. His Firstborn exists beyond death. They told me he had been killed, but he escaped somehow.*

I clenched my eyes shut. I tried to calm the rapid beating of my undead heart. *Bill is going to kill me...*

Or he might beat me like he did before...

Or he might be happy I survived and hug me. The truth was I didn't know how he would react.

Get a grip. It had been over seventy years. *Bill is dead.*

I peeked from under the bed.

The room was the same. However, I regretted my choice of pajamas. The cotton pajama shorts emblazoned with gray kittens and a matching tee-shirt would not offer much protection if someone came in and smashed the shutters.

My hands trembled. The front door's deadbolt was locked, wasn't it? Though it wasn't like a deadbolt would slow a century-old vampire who was capable of kicking the door off its hinges.

The deep voice shouted a blasphemy. Another shout. Higher, but it still sounded male. Another shouted profanity. I couldn't make out all the words.

Then a scream of agony. Higher, possibly female. Maybe two people were screaming!

If Bill wanted revenge, he might go after Derrik. I had to move. *Ensure Derrik's okay.* I dashed across the hall to his suite.

I pounded on his door and entered. Hugo's bed was

empty. I remembered he had taken his mother to morning Mass and ran into the connected coffinroom. Nothing was out of order. The heavy layers of velvet were draped around the oak coffin.

"Dear God, please be in there!" I knocked on the lid.

Derrik opened it. His mustache was protected by a leather and cotton snood, and his cheeks were shiny with cold cream which smelled of orange blossoms. "What's wrong?"

"Someone's screamed. I came to check on you."

Derrik patted my hand. "Just one of your day-terrors. If you'd take to sleeping in coffins like a normal vampire, nothing would wake you." He covered his mouth to stifle a yawn.

"How can you not have heard it?"

"Perhaps my closet might comfort you?" He said, "There's an extra quilt on the bench, my lamb."

He obviously wanted me to sleep and I wished hiding in Derrik's closet didn't appeal to me. When I was a girl on my bad days, I ended up in my closet. On the very worst, I ended up in his closet, which held the comforting scents of lavender, and orange-peel sachets between his suits, the cedar walls, and his stored earth. It almost reminded me of the mountain on which I was born and reborn.

Somewhere in the coven, the voice screamed again. This time pitched high with terror.

Half-happy I wasn't insane and half-terrified I was running into an unknown situation wearing kitty pajamas, I jumped to my feet. I dashed from the room, then the apartment. Derrik put on a robe and followed. "Norma, come back! For the love of God, stop running into danger."

"I've been sensing this all night!" I tapped my brow to drive the point home.

"You're not dressed!"

"I need to know what I'm sensing."

Glass shattered from down the hall. I bumped into

Ryan's shoulder as he came through his door. It felt like I ran into a wall. He took my arm to steady me.

"Stay with Derrik, something bad is happening," I shouted.

I slipped away from him before Derrik caught up to us. Other vampires and thralls spilled from their apartments in various states of undress.

I smelled blood as soon as I hit the stairwell. Fresh blood. Other vampires would be smelling it too. I raced up the flight of stairs, hand on the inner rail so I might not lose a step with the stairwell's rotation.

I passed the door on the third floor landing because footfalls dashed across the hallway above me.

I made the next turn and stopped. A beam of sunlight flooded in from an open window and on to the landing between floors.

I stared at the brilliant blue heel and polished leather of Xiao's shoes. And attached to the shoes, Xiao lay with a wooden stake protruding through his chest.

"Oh my God!" I screamed and pressed my back against the wall, carefully ducked under the beam of burning death pouring into the window. The right side of his beautiful face and right hand were burned. In his hand, he clenched a sticky piece of black lace. Bloody footsteps led up the stairs to the fourth-floor hallway.

"Norma?" Derrik called.

"I'm here. And Xiao. Be careful; there's a broken window, and light's coming in. He might be dead. Is the stake thing real?"

"What do you mean 'is the stake thing real?'" Derrik shouted. His panicked voiced seemed to echo all around me. Anyone who wasn't awake had to be now.

"Of course it's real. No species could survive getting a stake punctured through their heart," Ryan shouted up at me. "Is Xiao dead? Final dead?"

"I don't know but someone put a piece of wood in his chest! Xiao, come on, brother, wake up!"

A woman screamed and a man shouted. I was sure it was the voice I heard before, but couldn't identify the direction. Only it wasn't Derrik or Ryan's voices which were now at the doorway to the stairwell.

"He's burned! Get any strong thrall who can carry a stretcher. I'm afraid to move him alone."

"My son," Loretta screamed. "He's dying! I feel it!" Her white arm reached into the stairwell but was pulled back.

"Stop, there's a broken window. Norma was small enough to slip under it, but there's no room for us too," Derrik said.

"I can't breathe!" Loretta cried. "My son is in so much pain."

"If you want to help, get the damn stretcher from the clinic," I called. "And something to cover this window!"

"We're coming!"

Kuma and Bernie raced up the stairs with the stretcher.

"Get up the stairs while we move him, Norma," Kuma said.

I did as instructed.

Doing the best to keep his torso level, the two lifted Xiao on to the stretcher. Once the stretcher was out of the sun, I grabbed the corner.

Beside me, Bernie thought: *Xiao deserved what he got for attacking humans.*

I was so shocked by the fury, I almost lost my grip.

The lace fluttered from Xiao's hand to the floor. It was delicate like Loretta's style, but practically every vampire wore black lace some of the time, and many of the female thralls wore lacy slip-style dresses including Fern. I grabbed it and stuffed it in my pajama shorts waistband so not to lose it.

Ethan hurried over with a large piece of plywood

which covered his whole body and hammered the board over the open window. Something emanated from his mind, but I couldn't quite make it out over my own fear.

Loretta dashed up to the next landing. Derrik and Ryan were behind her. "My Firstborn!" She cradled Xiao's head to her breast. Charles held his wife and her offspring. "I feel him dying. He's hurt so terribly."

Agata hurried down the stairs. "Bring him to the infirmary. Norma, come along if you're willing."

"How do we know she didn't stake him?" Fern screeched.

I glanced at Fern's clothing. She wore black silk pajamas. They were tailored, not lacy.

"Lady Loretta, you should rip her limb from limb because what she did to Xiao. She should never have been made. Everyone says so."

Loretta's white face peered at me in a mask of fury. Loretta had always been kind, albeit distant with me, but she was also three centuries. It was hard to know what an older vampire would do, especially one in agony.

"Enough," Agata said. "Everyone calm yourselves. I need to remove the stake to verify the extent of the damage. Xiao might survive if we focus on saving him. Derrik, take Loretta to the parlor. Charles, Norma, come with me."

"Can I help?" Ryan asked.

"Yes, we might need you to hold him," Agata said.

Agata was smart. If Xiao met Final Death on the operating table, Charles would be there to witness we did all we could.

Chapter 5

10:45 AM

I FELT SOMETHING HEAVY AS I PEELED XIAO'S silk jacket off his limp frame. Since his shirt and undershirt were ruined, Agata cut them off.

I slipped my hand in the pocket and found an engraved bleeding blade. I expected it to be Xiao's, but when I turned it over a swirling script read *RJR*. The J was double the size of the two Rs. I recognized it immediately because other than the initials it was identical to mine. It was given to Ryan from Derrik on the day of his initiation. I wondered why Xiao would have Ryan's knife, but it wasn't the appropriate time to ask about that.

Though both men leaned heterosexual, eternity was a long time. Maybe they hooked up. Maybe Ryan wasn't attracted to Fern, but Xiao, who was coming into his vampire prowess. Perhaps, Ryan hooking up with his friends is where Derrik got the idea I hooked up with my friends. I left it in his pocket as I hung the jacket on the back of a chair.

Agata positioned Ryan at Xiao's feet and Charles at his shoulders. She prepared two injections and inserted the first needle into Xiao's neck.

At Agata's direction, I grabbed the box of pressure bandages. I had no idea how much this type of wound would bleed, but I would be prepared.

"Everyone ready?" Agata straightened her stance,

gripped the stake with both hands and pulled it out of Xiao's chest.

His eyes opened as he screamed. The iris on his burnt side looked milky. Charles and Ryan held him as his body convulsed. The iron tang of blood filled the air.

I kept the pressure on the bandage which became soaked under my fingers. Xiao's spattered lifeforce hypnotized me. My fangs extended from my gums, I willed them back. It didn't work. I felt the aching bloodlust I had known my first nights as a vampire. *Thank God, I drank from Kuma earlier.*

"Calm down, Xiao. Good, Son. Agata's here to help you," Charles said in a soothing manner. His fangs too had expanded. So had Agata's and Ryan's.

I feared a bloodbath if one of the older vampires lost control. Ryan and I would meet our final death and probably Xiao too.

Agata inspected the wound as she pushed around flesh and innards.

"Good, the heart was only grazed as was his lung. With enough blood we should be able to save him," she said. "I must clean and stitch the wounds. Charles, get the saline. Norma, would you mind cleaning up? This much blood is distracting."

Charles handed the saline to Agata who opened the bottle and rinsed the wound trying to wash away any loose slivers. I applied a sharp grapefruit cleaning spray on the blood on the floor to ease the tension, but kept my eyes on Agata who sutured the heart with absorbable thread.

I had started to mop the floor when Marion threw the door open and tracked through the place I had cleaned. "Why didn't you call me?"

Agata placed another pressure bandage. "No time. Emergency medical treatment is needed."

Marion rolled her shoulders back, turned up her collar, and placed her hands over her nose and mouth.

With both Charles and Ryan holding Xiao in a sitting position, Agata wrapped Xiao's torso with gauze. Once finished, Agata, Marion, Ryan, and Charles moved him onto a fresh bed. Agata gave him the second injection.

I grabbed the bloody sheeting, torn clothing, and used bandages. I double-bagged it in plastic. I re-mopped the floor.

"Xiao, honey, do you hear me?" Agata said.

He groaned.

"Xiao, your heart and left lung are damaged. You've second-degree burns on your hands and face. Do not move, but you must drink." Agata cut open her wrist and pressed it to his lips.

The smell of ancient blood added to the century-old blood. Memories rose in my mind of the hunts I went on with Bill before the coven took me away from him. He loved playing bloody cat and mouse games with his victims. I salivated and checked the clock. Though it seemed like hours had passed, it was only seconds. I cranked the air conditioning to circulate through the room and took the bloody sheets to the laundry. My fangs finally retracted.

When I returned, Agata had washed her wrist and bound it. With stored donated blood, she set up a transfusion IV system to drip the precious liquid into Xiao's arm. Charles dabbed a spicy-smelling unguent on Xiao's burnt face which made it much easier to breathe.

Xiao's eyes fell upon Marion. He opened his mouth. Only a wheezing gasp moved through his lips.

"It's all right, Xiao, can you lift a pen?" Marion took a pen from her pocket.

Xiao took it in his unburnt left hand.

"Who staked you?"

In messy handwriting with his nondominant hand, he scrawled: *Was trying … sun blinded me. Too much pain. Don't remember.*

"Was it Norma? She broke up that fight," Marion

asked. "And you have an issue with her as do we all."

"You have an issue with me?" I said sadly. I knew, of course, but it hurt to hear it. In the decades of my undead existence, Xiao had always been kind to me.

Charles glared. The pinched lines on his forehead and between his eyebrows from his days as a solider-turned-trapper drew deeper. After becoming a gentleman again, he kept his brown hair and mustache neat, but he never reached the refinement of his gentile wife. As he rubbed his left fist into his right palm, he looked not the gentleman at all.

I stopped cleaning and remained still, afraid he might rip my head off. It was better to show deference than quarrel with elder vampires. As progressive as the Seattle coven was, their ethics were still from a bygone era.

Xiao wrote: *Too short.*

"Her shade?" Marion asked.

"It wasn't Carlos!" I cried. "He went home hours ago."

Agata put up her hand. I fell silent. Marion moved away from the bed.

"Would you like Fern to visit you?" Agata asked.

No. Don't want her to see a monster.

"My poor little bunny, your wound should heal quickly if everyone donates a little blood. Maybe a few weeks, a month at most," Agata patted his leg. "Try and rest."

"What's this?" Marion asked.

My stomach dropped as Marion pulled Ryan's knife from Xiao's jacket pocket.

"RJR?" Marion said.

Agata lifted her hand in the air again. "There are too many people in this room. I have a patient. Norma, mind allowing us the use of your office for a chat?"

Chapter 6

11:17 AM

AGATA CAREFULLY LOCKED THE DOOR TO the infirmary and put up a sign: **Quiet. Patient Resting.**

I led the other vampires into my office. I quickly grabbed my discarded work clothes off the couch and tucked them into a file drawer so everyone could have a place to sit.

Without waiting for any politeness, Marion held out Ryan's knife. "So how do you explain this?"

"You're blaming me?" Ryan asked.

"Right now, I'm asking a question," Marion said.

"I lost it; Xiao must have found it."

"Where did you lose it?"

"If I knew, it wouldn't have been lost," Ryan said.

"Ryan didn't do it," I said quickly.

"How do you know that?"

"Because I heard footsteps running on in the hallway above, but I bumped into him when he came out of his apartment. Xiao also had this when I found him." I held out the lace.

"A piece of bloody lace?" Marion snatched it from my hand. "Do you know how many pieces of bloody lace are in this coven? Plus, you've been touching it. If you are the killer, we would not be able to use this to convict you."

I almost pointed out that now she touched it; it could

not be used to convict her either. As that was rash and ill-advised I did not. "I didn't want to lose any clues. Sorry."

"Are you hiding something? You seem to know where everyone was." Charles jabbed at me with his finger. "Were you out causing trouble like you did when you were young?"

That was an unfair question with no good answer, but I figured the truth was best. "No, I was in my room, I mean, Derrik's guest room, but I was awake."

"Why were you awake?" Marion hissed at me.

"A touch of insomnia. I was reading one of Derrik's trashy romances when I heard shouting. I ran to Derrik first."

"You always hide behind Derrik," Charles said. "And he spoiled you..."

Agata stood up. "Order."

Marion snapped her mouth shut. Charles's posture did not change, but he stopped speaking.

"This is the second time we have seen Xiao in the middle of violence within twenty-four hours. Are both quarrels related?" Agata asked the assembled vampires.

"Norma was involved both times too," Marion said.

"Indeed she was. Norma, why did you step into that first fight?" Agata asked.

"Xiao pushed Fern," I said.

Charles grabbed my wrist. "How vampires treat their thralls is none of your damn business, so answer Agata's question truthfully."

He couldn't read minds; he just wanted a better answer. I had always been a little scared of Charles. He accepted me in the coven only because his beloved Loretta did.

"Norma didn't lie. I would've sensed it," Ryan said.

"And why should we trust you?" Marion asked.

Agata cleared her throat. "Xiao might have laid there all day if Norma hadn't found him."

"Are you justifying her actions?" Marion asked.

Agata turned toward Marion without anger. "No. I am

obliged to know what she observed either in our reality or in her mind. Remove your hand, Charles, if you please. You forget yourself in your grief."

He didn't.

If I could have scooted toward Agata without losing any credibility, I would have. Since I couldn't, I did my best to remain outwardly calm. Ensuring I used the bloodlines, which vampires alleged were important, I said, "Yes, Charles, I'm sorry for embarrassing Xiao, Lady Loretta, and Lady Agata, and you and Jakub. I wouldn't ever want to cause pain to the vampires who raised me. I owe you all a great debt."

"Write to Xiao and my lady, if you please. You hurt them by making such scenes," Charles said, a little more calmly.

Loretta hurried into the room. He released my wrist as he stood. Everyone stood, except Agata.

Even in her fury, pain, and terror, every inch of Loretta looked soft with her wide-set eyes and strawberry hair. She wore scarlet lipstick and a pale pink blush and a long black, lacy gown from the era from which she was a young noblewoman. "Mother, will he ...?

"Your son should survive," Agata said. "I gave him a transfusion. Now we seek information so Marion might ascertain how it happened and who is to blame."

She slipped into her husband's arms who embraced her. They sat down beside each other.

"Thank God. When the pain left my heart, I feared the worse."

Derrik and Jakub trailed in after her. "We couldn't keep her away."

Agata waved them to sit.

Having the chance to escape from sitting beside Charles, I used the opportunity to sit between Derrik and Jakub. They wouldn't protect me from Charles any more than Agata had, but he would be less likely to grab me with

Derrik around.

"Good." Agata said. "Norma, I expect an answer if we could get through without all these interruptions: Why did you feel a need to step in?"

"Xiao, Bernie, and Ethan's emotions were ramping up. Xiao didn't even know he hurt Fern. He was just pushing away the hands that held him back from Ethan." Norma paused. "Marion, you may want to see if you can discover anything about the young man who ran away."

Marion crossed her arms. "Keep your nose out of it."

Derrik stiffened beside me. I wondered if he felt the same antagonism that I did or if he was purposely ignorant of it.

Jakub said softly, "With her past, Norma has an excellent nose for trouble. Have you discussed how she knew Xiao was in the hall?"

"No. If you please, dear heart," Agata said.

"The shouting. I was sure it was two men, maybe three. Maybe the third was a woman. I felt danger earlier. It weighed on my mind all night."

"Do you claim precognition?" Jakub's eyes immediately shifted to Derrik as if to ask is this was a new gift in the bloodlines.

"I claim I was tense. Probably, it was just my empathic gift. I felt like there was someone's anger coming from somewhere, but I couldn't sense where. Xiao argued with Ethan earlier about that man.

"Marion, maybe you should check with the IT department?"

"Who are you to tell me what to do?" Her voice was full of indignation. "I said, stay out of it."

"Please, listen. Xiao is our system administrator. That man had his phone in his hand. Ethan told me he snapped a picture. What if Xiao saw something strange on our network today? What if that's what all this is about?"

Charles made an inarticulate grumble under his breath.

Marion shot a false smile; her lips pinched into a thin white line. "It is something of a possibility."

Agata reminded everyone to donate blood, except me. I didn't weigh enough. And she warned Loretta to be extra careful. Slender and petite as she was, she was just below the current weight standards. The vampires left to give blood, dress for their jobs, or sleep as their schedules dictated.

"Ryan, could you wait? I wanted to ask you something," I whispered.

With his hand on the doorknob, he said with a voice full of exhaustion, "What?"

"You lied about why Xiao had your knife."

"So?"

"Why lie when I can see you're lying?"

"Because I see no reason to tell *a girl* about my personal life."

"Xiao was staked. And Marion's going to look into it," I whispered.

"What's it to you?" Without waiting for a reply, Ryan said, "You aren't one of the coven elders or Dick Tracy. I don't have to answer your questions."

"But..." I didn't have a real response.

"Cleaning messes hardly qualifies you as a detective. Let Marion handle it. Leave me alone. I've had enough of your and Derrik's nagging tonight." He slammed the door as he left.

I sank onto my couch.

Ryan had lied. I was sure about that. Yet I had to be careful not to jump to conclusions. One of the many dangers of telepathy was hearing half-thoughts from several people smashed together and thinking it was truth. After I came to the coven, it took me several months to learn to quiet the noise and I didn't always succeed.

I was angry that I had promised to write apology letters. *Why did I do that?*

Charles was pissed and it was the quickest way to placate him. I didn't trust anyone under this roof except Derrik and Pascaline not to hurt me.

I opened my desk drawer and pulled out a box of personalized stationery which Pascaline had given to me. I stared at the ivory paper emblazoned with my initials and a tiny golden butterfly. The blank page loomed in front of me. I hated not knowing what to write.

I'm so sick of vampires and their rules. Ryan's right. What can I do, except let Marion work?

Without writing a word, I stood, took off my pajamas and changed into my jeans and a Norma's Cleaning Service tee. I gathered my Sabbath clothing.

I went down to the laundry, swapped the formerly-bloody sheets to the dryer and laundered my skirt and blouse and pajamas. It felt good to put away my "vampire costume."

Once the cycle was over, I shoved the pajamas in the dryer, folded the sheets and hung my skirt and blouse on my office's shower curtain rod. If they weren't dry by the time Carlos arrived, I could hang them properly next week when I visited my office and did my bookkeeping.

I tried to write again:

My honored brother Xiao,

I'm sorry I reacted in a way unbecoming of a vampire during the fellowship and embarrassed you by stepping into a quarrel...

I crushed the sheet of paper. Vampires were never fooled by insincerity. I would write them later.

Derrik met me in the hall with a flinty hard stare in his blue eyes, but his wrath failed to hide abject fear. I witnessed that same expression the night he and Xiao took me from Bill.

Derrik fit the obsessive-compulsive vampire mythos

too well; he hated when everything was spiraling out of control. He had dressed to his waistcoat — which he still considered undressed — and had a bandage on his wrist, but that meant he was not planning on returning to his coffin any more than I was.

"What did you say to Ryan?" He asked.

I sighed. "Come in my office or let's go in yours."

We went in his. Another sign that he was freaked. I sank into one of his matching Victorian leather chairs. He sat on the other, not sitting back or loosening his posture.

I pressed my hands on my jeans. "Xiao had Ryan's knife on him. I wanted to know why, because the reason he told Marion was, at least, half a lie."

"Did you read his mind?" Derrik bit off each word.

"No. Or I didn't mean to anyway. I was trying to say the right thing to Charles so he wouldn't tear my head off."

"Charles was just emotional. Loretta was in agony. You would understand if you lost an offspring."

Derrik was speaking of his own loss, but since he would never say it by name, anger boiled in my chest.

"I will never have offspring, will I? Agata said I can't even donate blood for Xiao."

Derrik's expression became pained by my words. I slipped my mind open so he could feel my emotions which I knew was cruel to do to an empath. I couldn't stand knowing I was an abusive jerk, so I slammed it shut and used my words.

"Charles squeezed my wrist. I'm not hurt, but by what right did he have to touch me? I'm to write Loretta and Xiao apology notes because I'm such a coward with other vampires of my own family," I said.

Derrik looked at his feet. A lock of golden hair fell out of place. "Ryan's stomping around. He won't speak to me. Hugo is still out with his mother, but not answering his phone. The day grows late. And you will be leaving as soon as Carlos arrives?"

As if struck by a new thought, Derrik tilted his head. His shoulders stiffened. He stood up and pulled me to my feet. He kissed my cheek. "Maybe, that's for the best. Yes, it's for the best if he comes early. Be safe."

He opened the door to his office.

"You be safe too," I said, both confused and hurt by the sudden dismissal.

The door closed. I glanced back through the window. Derrik sat at his desk and wept into one of his many lace-edged handkerchiefs.

Chapter 7

Noon

UNSURE IF I SHOULD TURN AROUND AND hug Derrik or what to do next, I returned to my own office. I reclined on my couch and texted Carlos. **Xiao was staked.**

About ten minutes passed before he replied. I wasn't surprised. It wasn't during normal work hours and most days I'd be in bed at this hour. He was probably playing with his cats.

Carlos: **You OK?**

Me: **Yeah. But I've got to figure this out.**

Carlos: **What do you mean you've got to figure it out?**

Me: **Figure out who did this.**

Carlos: **Aren't we working tonight?**

Me: **If any clients come in, take the job. But Marion found Ryan's knife on Xiao. I can't leave Derrik in a bind.**

Carlos: **Sounds like Ryan's in the bind.**
Maybe it would be best if you went home?

He sent a gif of a person banging his head against the wall. He was right: the coven did make me crazy.

Me: **I need to stay. If something happens to Ryan, Derrik will do something stupid. Keep the van, go on jobs if you feel like it. If not, enjoy some PTO.**

Carlos: **What am I going to do with paid time off?**

Me: **Teach your cats new tricks?**
Remember to make videos and make millions on YouTube.

Carlos didn't respond right away, but the ellipsis which meant he was typing. The ellipsis disappeared, then reappeared. Finally, I received two letters.

Carlos: **OK.**

Me: **I might not have made it, if not for Derrik. I can't leave him. He's crying.**

Carlos: **I said, OK.**

I looked around trying to think about what a detective needed. *iPhone, paper, pen, I know!* I grabbed a handful of plastic baggies and a pair of tweezers.

Thinking about my advice to Marion, I took the stairs to Jakub's thrall, Summer Dahlgard's apartment on the 6th floor. As I climbed the steps, another thought slipped into my mind. Summer and Xiao worked together in the IT department. *What if they had a fight at work and Summer staked him?*

I trembled as I walked along the hall to Summer's apartment. A chill ran down my spine. *If Summer's the killer, am I stepping into a trap?* With every step, my feet grew heavier. I wondered if I should turn back.

I was disappointed to see a "do not disturb" sign on her doorknob. *Okay, talking to Summer will have to wait.*

Vampires were always respectful of those who donated blood. If Summer had staked Xiao, the "do not disturb" sign would allow her to escape from Seattle. She'd have all day to get on a plane or train. After a few seconds entertaining *Great Escape* scenarios, I thought logically. Moving was a pain and staking a vampire seemed excessive when Summer might have easily asked Jakub for mediation or even a new job.

I sat on the top step of the landing and opened my notebook and wrote: knife.

Marion had Ryan's knife ... and a stupid lie of a story.
Lace.

How would I discover who wore the lace? Most vampires wore lace sometimes, so did many of the thralls. Marion had lace too.

Footsteps.

Someone was running on the floor above, but I had no idea how to figure out who it might have been. *Unless someone saw something?*

Blood.

There was blood splatter on the carpet.

Maybe I can deduce the size of the shoe if I retraced the path. I might even be able to get a shoe print! I glanced at my phone. I only had a few hours before the custodian arrived and washed the carpet.

I ran to grab a tape measure and returned to where I found Xiao. As I climbed the steps, I shuddered in fear the killer was still about.

Blood stained the wallpaper and soaked into the stairwell carpets. The largest stains were where Xiao had lain. None of the prints were full shoe marks. Looking at the splotches annoyed me. I saw plenty of blood at work, but I didn't know what the marks and patterns meant. "I should have watched more CSI," I muttered.

I used the tape measure to keep the scale accurate of each blob as I took a picture and wrote down the measurements. The trail of bloody blobs moved upward. Careful not to step in them, I followed them to the fourth-floor landing. The blobs grew smaller until they all but disappeared except the drops and smudges on the wallpaper.

Did the killer exist on the fourth floor? Or maybe, they used the fourth floor to escape and circle back around? Or had we spread the blood when we transported Xiao to the clinic. I thought about *A Scandal in Bohemia* when Sherlock told Watson, "You see what you do not observe."

Maybe that's the problem. I saw the blood, but I missed how to see. I had no idea about blood splatter. Maybe Ryan's right and I should be leaving this to Marion.

I sat on the stairs above the blood and pondered my next move.

A low voice angrily hissed, "I told you to leave him alone."

I pressed my back against the wall, trying to be as small as possible. The voice sounded close. I wondered if they were right on the other side of the landing door. With the hope I might identify them, I opened my mind. Mistake! There were too many murmuring voices and inner fears. I closed my mind, clearing it. I took a deep breath. I had to be more careful.

"Since when do you tell me..." The second voice wavered in its fury and rose to a fevered pitch. "What do you know about anything?"

The second voice echoed. I couldn't tell if it was coming from below or above. My skin tingled as bloody sweat rose to the surface. I peeked over the banister, first looking down. I couldn't see anyone. I looked up. Still no one.

"I know about vampires, I've lived with them," the first voice hissed. "You only think you know."

Dread filled my soul. I didn't recognize either voice. *What if I was just hearing thoughts?* I needed to discover who spoke, but my feet refused to budge. The slam of the heavy metal fire door echoed across the stairs. That sounded like it was below me. Where had they gone? I released a breath I didn't know I held in.

My silent footsteps padded downward, I went to the next door and peeked my phone down the hall. I snapped a quick picture with the camera. The hallway was empty. I checked the other floors, snapping photos along the way. On the ground floor, the picture contained the edge of the security desk at the end of the hall. Keith Lloyd would be on duty this time, and he would have been at the main entrance during the Sabbath. If it had been someone who didn't reside here, they would've signed in and out! I hurried to the desk but realized I only overheard a snippet of conversation.

"Hey, Keith."

His blue eyes peered over the screen and wiped his large ruddy nose. Most of the time his job was pretty dull, and he passed the hours with movies. He sat at the front desk all day. While few people came to the coven during the day, packages were delivered, and he met plumbers, electricians and other service people who kept standard business hours.

"Hello, Norma." He jumped to his feet but kept his neck and chest protected. His voice was smaller than it should be for a man who was built like a brick house and wore all black to his boots and cowboy hat. "Is Xiao all right?"

"Yes, he's expected to pull through."

"Thank God," he said softly. The fear in his voice was apparent. "Do you think Marion wants my blood?"

"Not unless you're offering."

"Do you know if Lady Agata wants me to resign?"

I thought it was nice Keith thought to ask of Xiao before his job. "I doubt it, but you'll have to ask her."

"Maybe I should resign."

"I don't know if anyone blames you. The assailant might've come to the Sabbath as an initiate."

"Really?" Keith's eyes lit up with hope. It might be a tedious job, but it paid a living wage and full benefits. He had a wife who worked part-time and two school-age kids at home. I could understand why he didn't want to lose his situation.

"Does Lady Agata want my blood?"

I sighed. "Why do you think everybody wants your blood?"

"You're vampires."

"Good point. Can I see who signed in?"

"Sure. Marion looked too."

I scanned the list. Maria left four hours before Xiao was attacked.

The Bellevue Coven Group left three hours before Xiao was attacked. Though Roger had stayed.

Gavin Sean Tupper did not sign out, but by the speed he left the parlor, it might have been an oversight. Ethan's last name was also Tupper. That couldn't be a coincidence. *But why did Ethan lie?* I would need to question him or maybe Marion would. Maybe that proved Ethan's innocence. Why would he lie if he was planning to stake a vampire?

As I looked at the sign-in sheet, I noticed a piece of lace in the garbage. Was it the same one? Why hadn't Marion looked closer? I took a quick picture of the sign-in sheet and the garbage can. "Can I take the lace?"

Keith shrugged. "I guess so."

I didn't know what the clue meant, but I was pretty sure it had to be a clue. *Why would Marion throw it away?* I reached into the trash with my tweezers, carefully collected the lace, and sealed it into a baggie. The hum and slurping sound of a carpet cleaner caught my attention.

I PEEKED BACK INTO THE STAIRWELL AND slowly ascended the steps. Between the third and fourth floors, Cameron, the custodian, washed the carpet with his earbuds in. The bloody footprints had disappeared. Even if I didn't understand blood splatter, I was glad I recorded the evidence.

The butler didn't do it, I thought. Though Cameron was not a butler; the coven didn't have a butler. I doubted he would stake Xiao. Most of his hours were during the day.

Cameron's blue button-down shirt stuck to his sweaty back and rotund paunch. *We really needed to get a new air conditioning system.* His thinning dark hair was held back by a headband to keep the perspiration out of his dark brown eyes. Cameron was so efficient. Normally, he just swept and mopped the tile floors and vacuumed the carpets after the Sabbath.

I waved. He returned a worried wave and popped his earbud out.

"Hi, Cam. What are you listening to?" I asked

"Oh, hello, *Milkman* by Anna Burns. It won the Booker last year."

"I haven't read it yet." I put my hands in my pockets.

"It's pretty good." He glanced over his shoulder. I sensed his vague distrust of the vampires. Normally, he only dealt with Keith. Sometimes Agata or Marion.

To put him at ease, I smiled with my mouth closed so he did not see my fangs. "Seen anything unusual around?"

He looked at the blood-filled reservoir of the carpet cleaner and back at me.

"Besides all the blood on the carpet," I amended.

"Not anything I ought to tell you. Why aren't you in your coffin? Don't you know this window was broken?"

"Did you hear Xiao was staked this morning?"

"The vampire from Apartment 403?"

"Yeah," I said.

"Oh, my God, no. I was just told to clean up this mess. Will he survive?"

"Lady Agata gave him a blood transfusion. He's expected to pull through. I'm trying to find clues."

"Was it a hunter?" Cameron whispered.

"We have no idea yet."

"It's not my place to say, Miss Norma, but go to your coffin where you're safe."

I nodded demurely. "I will. But are you sure you didn't see anything?"

Cameron frowned.

I gently reminded him of my age. "I get you weren't

even alive back then, so you probably don't know this, but when the coven found me, Xiao covered my eyes against the violence. Derrik raised me, but the other vampires helped."

"So it takes a village, even with vampires." He glanced over his shoulder, then down the stairwell and up it. He lowered his voice. "You didn't hear it from me, but some days, I see the woman leave unit 403 while, presumably, the vampire sleeps."

"And goes where?"

"Not my place to say, but she's dressed like she needs more attention than a single vampire can provide."

"Thanks, Cam."

NOT SURE WHAT TO DO NEXT, I WANDERED to Derrik's office and knocked on the door. He answered wiping his cheeks with his handkerchief. The circles under his bloodshot eyes betrayed how tired he was. His cheeks were bloodstained where tears had fallen. Small piles of burnt matches lay on his desk. "Has Carlos arrived?"

"He's not coming."

"What?" He lit a match and blew it out.

"I gave him the night off. I'm staying with you."

"You trying to sell me a dog?"

More Victorian phrasing. "No."

"It's safer if you go." He measured and trimmed the unburnt part of the match, and put it in the appropriate pile.

"Yep, probably. But you need me, and since you don't ever come to my house, I'm staying with you." I paused, realizing I was breaking vampire social code by staying longer than the invitation had plainly stated. "Oh. I guess I wasn't invited. Well, I'll stay in Pascaline's or my office if you're tired of house guests. But I won't leave the coven till I figure out what happened."

"Even though you're leaving money on the table?"

I regretted ever thinking money was more important than what was going on with Derrik. "Yep. Are those for the ferry in my room or something else?"

He lit another match and stared at the flame. "I don't know yet." He blew out the match and repeated his procedure. "My home is your home. You can stay as long as you want."

I figured now I could ask for his help. I told him about the conversation I had heard on the stairs. "What do you think it meant?"

"It might have meant nothing. Or it might have been the homicidal maniac and his accomplice. There's no way to know, but I thank God you had enough sense to hide."

"I also talked to Keith and Cam. Keith's afraid he will get fired or bled."

Derrik's emotional state didn't stop him from cracking a smile. "Of course, he does. All vampires do is bleed people and write checks."

"Cam didn't see anything, but he's already cleaning up the blood. So I got these pictures before he did." I showed Derrik my photos and notes. "I don't understand blood splatter, but I put together the evidence. What do you know about this? Marion won't listen to me, but she'd listen to you."

He shook his head. "I've never worked on anything like blood splatter." He turned my phone in his hands. "All I see is blobs. Well, this one kind of looks like a dog."

"Yeah, that's what I saw too. What about the lace or Ryan's knife? If..."

"You must believe in our coven brother."

"Says the lawyer," I said.

Derrik pinched the bridge of his nose. "Ryan's my creation. He is as close to you in bloodline as I am."

"But he was lying."

"What warning did I give you about these gifts?"

He had instructed me in all aspects of vampire powers,

but I knew the answer he wanted. "Many things go on people's heads. The innocent can feel guilty, and everybody justifies everything to themselves."

"Yes. If you want to play Miss Marple, keep your observant nature on figuring out who hurt Xiao, not Ryan's activities," Derrik said.

"I was trying to be Sherlock Holmes."

"Miss Marple doesn't insult her friends."

"Good point. I'll be Miss Marple," I said. "If a client came to you with these clues, what would you do?"

"All my clients want is contracts, wills, patent, or immigration paperwork."

"You've still never tried a criminal case? Not ever?"

"The closest I ever did to any criminal proceeding was bail coven members out of jail before they were immolated. We always settled out of court. But I haven't had to do that in over sixty years because your business ensures no vampire is in that predicament."

"What about Bill?"

"That was a different situation." He sighed and rubbed his eyes. His throat hitched as if he were about to cry again. Noon was late for Derrik. Since he rose at 6:30 PM, he went to bed most days by 10 am.

"You look exhausted," I said.

"I'm only out of my coffin because I can't sleep, knowing you're running around half-cocked. I'm too old to have such poor sleep hygiene, but you've too much Vampire William in you."

"Even now, it's dangerous to show it."

"I'll stay in and do an Internet search about blood splatter if it helps you sleep," I said.

"It would help me sleep if you would sleep like a normal vampire," Derrik said.

73

Chapter 8

12:37 PM

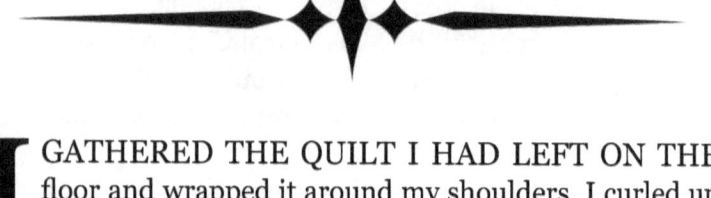

I GATHERED THE QUILT I HAD LEFT ON THE floor and wrapped it around my shoulders. I curled up on the daybed, trying to let sleep find me, but knowing it wouldn't. I must find a reasonable suspect. *There are too many people in the coven to suspect everyone.* And I wasn't even looking at the Bellevue vampires. *Should I suspect them too? Even though they left before the attack? No. That doesn't make sense.*

Marion's boyfriend had stayed, but why would he hurt Xiao? For Marion? Xiao and Marion were friends and siblings under Loretta. It wasn't logical.

Agata or Jakub had no reason to kill Xiao. If they decided he was a liability, they could just kick him out of the coven—*unless they didn't want to deal with the hassle.*

Don't be dumb, Norma! Agata saved Xiao and she would never want to get that much blood on the stairwell carpet.

Loretta and Charles loved their son, didn't they? What if only Loretta loved him? What if their familial love has been subverted into something else? It made Charles a suspect. *Focus.* Charles was there when Agata removed the stake. He called him son. *And I have no reason to believe Loretta and Charles are unhappy.*

Come on, think! Who else might have a beef with

Xiao?

Derrik? I squeezed my arms tightly forcing the idea out of my head. Xiao and Derrik were friends. I couldn't think of a single reason except he had two disappointing offspring. That had nothing to do with Xiao. Moreover, he was in his coffin when the screaming started.

What if it's something darker?

Compared to Loretta and Charles, Pascaline and Derrik had few offspring. Pascaline's only progeny, Alice, had married out of the coven. Bill was dead. Half the coven hated me. Ryan was behind on his dues. Their limb might be pruned. Who would want that? Loretta? Charles? One of their many children? For what purpose?

I couldn't think of a motive and had no time for paranoia or strange theories.

Fern? She had access to Xiao and was quick to put the suspicion on me. And Cam suggested she was having an affair. Who was the affair with?

Ryan? No, not Ryan.

Derrik was right. I should come home more often. At least I would know who is sleeping with who.

What about the other thralls? Bernie had been furious with Xiao and, of course, Ethan lied about knowing Gavin Sean Tupper.

Not getting anywhere with my circling thoughts, I went into the living room and waited on the couch for Hugo. Vampire Mass on Saturday night/Human Mass on Sunday mornings made for a long night.

I waited until he opened the front door.

"Hi, Hugo," I said softly so as not to startle him. "Did you and Maria have a nice time?"

"What are you doing up?" He sat across from me removed his shoes and socks and massaged his feet. "Whatever happened to Xiao had to be an accident. You've nothing to worry about."

"I don't see how getting staked could've been an accident. But I really wanted to ask you about something I heard."

"What's that, honey? I really need to get to bed. My sleep schedule is so messed up."

Jeez, could Derrik have a more compatible thrall? "Is Ryan having an affair?"

Hugo gestured to lower my voice; he glanced at the door to the suite. "No, of course not. But if he was, he wouldn't tell me about it."

"Derrik wouldn't judge if Ryan had an affair with another vampire," I said.

"And you wouldn't be asking questions if you thought it was an affair with another vampire." Hugo leaned back and gave me a half-hearted smile. "Derrik's having trouble keeping up. Hell, I'm having trouble keeping up, and I spent my youth in the world. But you need to help me take care of him and you asking questions about Ryan isn't helping anyone."

Hugo risked life and limb both as a racial and sexual minority marching for civil rights. Even at sixty and off his regular sleep schedule, he had an air of resilience younger men didn't. I thought back to the earlier conversation and asked, "You don't regret being here?"

"Of course not. Sometimes I wish I could retire to the suburbs, maybe one of the islands. I'm getting tired of city life. I just want to lie in the sun, have a few drinks." His expression seemed farther away.

"Well, you can grab a nonstop flight to Honolulu or even take a drive to Westport."

"Not with Derrik."

"No. Even if he could go, he'd stay here," I said.

"All I have is a few work friends and Mama's church friends who think it's so exciting they know a gay person when thirty years ago they told her to disown me."

"I'm sorry."

"Don't be. I'm glad times are changing. The optimist in me thinks it's for the better."

I wondered if Hugo knew about meetups to find traveling companions or even Tinder and Grinder for less than platonic relations. Vampires weren't necessarily monogamous with their human companions, but I didn't want to give bad advice. The condo was in Derrik's name as Derrik purchased it before Hugo was alive and would reside there long after he was dead. If he stayed, Derrik would take care of him and his aging mother until their natural deaths. If Hugo chose to leave Derrik, he got a severance package, but unless Hugo had been stashing the money he saved on rent into investments so he could purchase his own house, he might feel stuck in the situation.

"Why don't you want to be a vampire?" I asked.

"Being a vampire isn't everything. In a few decades, I'll be dead. But you'll still be here — worrying about global warming and taking care of Derrik who is falling back into his former era."

"Why'd you become a thrall?"

"*Así es la vida.*" (This is life.)

"You think Derrik's issues go deeper than old slang?"

"He worries he might need torpor before Pascaline wakes," Hugo said.

"I'll ensure his wishes are met," I said.

"That's what I told him. He could not ask for a more devoted coven sister."

"Do you think if he's falling backward enough to..." I left the question unasked. Hugo would fill in the blanks.

"He might turn his back on Ryan, or even you, if he thought you two acted in a way which would give people to think the coven was a place of decadence."

"I can't believe that."

"Why not? He did it before with William."

I opened my mouth wanting to defend Derrik, but no sound came out.

"That's why he nags you two so much. He fears Ryan is getting deeper into debt. And he fears for you. No other coven will accept you."

He patted my shoulder, set his shoes under the coat tree, and reminded me that staying up all day worrying didn't help anyone, least of all the worrier.

Chapter 9

1 PM

ONCE HUGO RETIRED, I RETURNED TO MY old room and opened the closet door. It almost smelled like Christmas. Winter-weight suits, rain jackets, and sweaters hung on wooden hangers, each one had an orange peel and cinnamon sachet. On the floor, boots in neat racks, each pair with appropriate cedar shoe or boot forms. The shelf above held three plastic banker boxes. The first was marked William T. Caruso/Ryan R. Jones; the middle was marked Norma M. Rollins; the final one marked Derrik Miller et all. *Derrik might be annoyed if I look through his boxes without permission.* In truth, I feared what I might find in the boxes. I didn't like to think about the time before Derrik loved me.

I measured my shoe, Hugo's size 11 and Derrik's size 10 1/2, then studied the bloody blobs on my phone again. The splotches still didn't look like shoe prints, but I saw the one Derrik thought looked like a dog. Another was shaped like a bunny and another like a sailboat.

Deciding I could always ask for forgiveness, I pulled Derrik's box down. It was his paperwork as Jakub's thrall, his education, his and Pascaline's marriage license, American citizenry and initiation paperwork. There were also contracts between him and his thralls each perfectly labeled.

The official paperwork was not nearly detailed enough to describe the adventure. Derrik was an eighteen-year-old factory worker in smog-filled London working twelve-hour nights for meager meals and a flea and lice-ridden hotbed who answered an advertisement for an able-bodied man. He escorted Jakub, Agata, Pascaline, and Loretta to America. Other than a little seasickness, the journey went smoothly. The women slept in boxes of French furniture. The two men were content in each other's company: Jakub the mentor; Derrik, the pupil.

He undertook the transformation to turn himself into a gentleman vampire with a good lady vampire wife. His common sense was of a former era, he was not ready for the thrilling force of nature known as Vampire William T. Caruso.

THE SHARED BOX FOR BILL AND RYAN WAS much lighter than Derrik's personal files. Each held the carbon copy of their initiation paperwork, portraits, and letters. Bill's space in the file box was thicker as it contained notes of Bill's experiments. The final file was Bill's exile and execution. I touched the file, but not ready to relive my rebirth and creator's death, I did not remove it from the box. Instead, I looked at the carbon copies of the initiation paperwork. Bill's final photograph taken in the 1930s was in black and white. Ryan's taken in the '80s was in color.

Derrik altered both men for reasons of affection. He and Bill were lovers during the initiation period and the fourteen years after. Ryan joined the coven as an initiate and connected with Derrik as a friend. By his personal notes, Derrik found them both physically attractive — though they couldn't have looked more different than each other. Ryan was a slenderly-built Black man of 185 pounds, six-foot-two; Bill had been a brawnier White man of 211 pounds and only five-ten. (Though in my mind, Bill towered over me, and

Ryan never does.)

They were both intelligent and well-regarded in their chosen fields. His two offspring were older than he had been when changed, so they had made their own lives outside of being vampires.

However unsimilar the two men were, Charles, Loretta, Pascaline, and Xiao, all bore witness how Ryan Robert Jones would never act with the impudence of William Thomas Caruso. Ryan was steady, respectful, kind. He had all the qualities to be trusted as a vampire.

When introduced to Ryan, Derrik had called me a "beloved mistake of his firstborn." It crushed me then. It crushed me now. However, as was expected, I came to Ryan's initiation and welcomed my honored brother into the coven on the night of his first Death and Rebirth.

I TOUCHED THE FILE HOLDING BILL'S EXILE and execution again. I didn't want to open it. I knew I would. Inside was a transcript of the discussion and meeting minutes.

The first page was a semi-false account of my Rebirth.

William: During my experiment in order to dominate humanity and end all wars, I have calculated the blood flow and the time of death on several body parts. I forced vampire blood into seventy-three patients through a golden cup. Unlike patients 001 to 072, Subject 073 transformed. Unfortunately, Subject 073 is a fourteen-year-old female.

I tried to terminate her during the transformation, but she is extremely clever, has Derrik's knightly soul and mind reading abilities. Norma is my creation, and I cannot destroy her. I am a father again.

I RECALLED THE LAST NIGHT OF MY LIFE AS easily as I remembered the previous night of undeath. There was no golden cup.

A boy from my class, Teddy Hunter, and I chased each other in a game of kissing flashlight tag with four other kids, pairing up boys and girls. Cold hands — too big to be Teddy's — gripped my arms. My first thought was the sheriff had caught us. Branches whipped past in frenzied movement as I flew underneath a dark shape. I was dropped onto the floor of somewhere cold and dark. I screamed when I saw the vampire's fangs. I tried to protect my throat with my arms. I struck him with my flashlight in the face which split open his lip. He yanked the flashlight from my hand, held me down.

He ripped off my shoe and bobby-sock and bit into my heel. I fought back, wildly kicking. "So, my Achilles, you have fight like the mythical one. I'm glad ... it's always better if you fight." He bit into my leg.

Tears streamed down my cheeks as my muscles spasmed. I would die with sin in my heart. I stole $3.00 from my mother's purse and smoked cigarettes with her friends. I kissed Teddy several times. I had been covetous and lustful.

He loosened his grip, I twisted and with my free leg, kicked the vampire. I twisted around and elbowed the vampire in the chest. Agonizing pain radiated into my arm, but I was free again. Ignoring the throbbing, I punched him squarely on his mouth. Blood sprayed onto my face. My eyes teared, burning with fiery blood. My lips tasted like copper.

I felt light-headed. With one final burst of strength, I lunged and bit into his hand. Blood rose in my mouth. He slapped me away.

"Spit! Vomit if you have to." He patted my back. "Come on, spit." I tried to spit. He wrapped his arms around me and pushed on my sternum. "Vomit. You must vomit! Don't swallow."

My ribs cracked as he squeezed harder.

I remembered screaming as he continued the Heimlich maneuver. Songs of death entered my body. I felt strange, a sort of giddiness. Cold darkness pressed in on me. Gloom parted. My vampire eyes could see in the dark as easily if it were day. Dead bodies littered the floor of the wooden barn. Pigeons sat in the rafters. Rats scurried among the hay. More bodies were stacked against the northern wall. Each corpse was mutilated in a different way. I knew I should be afraid, but all I felt was thirst and a strange dissatisfaction the vampire who stood above me was not named Dracula, but Bill.

"You'll be my death, girl, but you're my Firstborn. You've no idea what eternity means, but neither did I — and no program could explain it." He helped me to my feet, licked a handkerchief and washed the blood from my face.

He gestured toward the bodies. "I am experimenting with the best way to make a real vampire — not the weak ones in the city — with you and others like you I plan to overcome humanity in order to stop all war. You see my failures rotting. You're my first success. Honestly, I only planned to see the rate of blood loss via the Achilles, but you, Norma Mae Rollins, have fight."

I choked as my tongue relearned what it knew in life. My throat parched. I ached. I had seen lots of movies — she knew the ache was for blood. "I'm so thirsty, please... Mr. Caruso?"

"I'll get you blood soon. Remain still."

I ran my tongue over my teeth. *Where are my fangs?*

"You don't have fangs yet. They'll grow in the next few days."

"I want to go home."

"Listen. I'm the only one who's safe for you. You'd kill your mother. If the other vampires discover what I've done, they'll kill us both. I must teach you to survive before we're caught." He smiled. Danger excited him, just as kissing Teddy had excited me. I knew it somehow without being told. I wished I didn't.

I took a step back. "Why, Mr. Caruso?"

He tightened the grip on my shoulders "Call me Bill ... or even Dad. Before I was a vampire, I had two sons. I was a father. A good father. Your birth father died in World War II; my boy died in Korea. You obviously need a father, so you'll be my third child." He finished swiping dirt off my skirt, blouse and scratched hands as if to prove he was trustworthy. "I wonder if it means anything you lived fourteen years and I forty-one before our rebirths."

It sounded like a coincidence, but I didn't say anything. Dracula didn't take kindly to those who disagreed with him. (Nor from what I had seen did my friends' fathers. And I would soon learn Bill didn't allow defiance either.)

I clutched my stomach. The thirst drove nails into me.

He lifted my chin. "As you see my thoughts, I see yours. I won't censure your disbelief. My maker believes in numerology. Like you, I think it's a load of dung, but it explains many coincidences. I also looked at films and books in the beginning. I'm not like the others. See in my mind, if you can."

My throat felt like sand; I wanted a sip of blood so badly. "I'm thirsty."

"Do as I say and I'll give you blood."

I tried to read Bill's mind and saw several other vampires from several different nationalities; the women were beautiful and the men handsome. (I didn't know about gender fluidity back then.) He despised them. Two men stood out.

"Your creator is Derrik Miller?"

Another stupid name for a vampire! "He looks like an old-timey movie villain... the other man..."

Bill squeezed my hand uncomfortably. "What other

man?"

"Larry." *Larry? That's the worse name yet.* "He looks young but is older than you and Derrik. You two had a fight?"

"Enough. I wanted to show you Derrik, but Larry is important to me too. I knew you'd be a quick study. If you were a decade older, you would've been a fine vampire."

Only from Bill did I ever learn what it was to be a vampire like the ones from movies. I often wanted to hate him, but I only feared his mercurial nature which was easily provoked, and the images I saw in his head as the nights grew longer and colder.

FOR MY ILLEGAL CREATION AND HIS experimentation on 130 humans over the course of the summer, seven vampires found him guilty/zero found him innocent/Derrik abstained. Their rules dictated he must be exiled from the coven.

They didn't want to kill him, however, until as the report read:

William made a vocal outburst denigrating the lifestyle of coven vampires, showed concern we would all be destroyed by atomic bombs, and left laughing like a mad man.

Agata motioned to execute Vampire William for the good of all our kind because, he planned to keep killing and if caught, he would not hesitate to divulge the coven's presence to humans.

Charles seconded the motion.

The coven voted with her. Derrik abstained again. A note was made about how he was overcome with emotion.

The next page was a transcript of the discussion about what to do with *the girl.*

Jakub: We must not let the girl roam Issaquah alone. She might further shame the coven with her

geographical proximity to Bellevue.

Pascaline: William's apartment is vacant and his thrall, Aldo, is without a vampire. The girl might reside there. We might keep an eye on her in order to avoid a hasty decision.

This led to a long discussion about raising children and some of the horrors that Charles and Derrik experienced when they were of apprentice age. Agata had raised five human children and didn't want more. She had no idea what a girl of the modern age might need.

Jakub motioned to execute the girl along with William. As stated in the bylaws all of William's assets would return to the coven.

Agata seconded it.

Derrik: Wait! The girl is of my bloodline. I will take responsibility for her.

Pascaline: Please have compassion for Derrik's feelings. I motion to allow the girl to exist if she resides with Derrik.

Agata renounced her original support for execution and seconded this proposal.

Agata, Pascaline, Loretta, Alice, and Derrik voted to let me continue. Jakub, Charles, and Xiao abstained their vote until they discovered if I was deranged. The final page was a description of Bill's execution. According to the documents, he was dismembered and shackled to the roof of the barn with a chain made of silver. The coven burnt the barn insuring there was nothing but ash. I believed that to be the truth, but on occasion, I still see him, when I close my eyes.

"I SENSE DERRIK GETTING CLOSER," BILL said. "We should see the headlights soon."

"Then we should run."

Bill smiled, but some dark emotion swirled around his

eyes. "Look!"

Two sets of headlights turned upon the gravel road to the barn.

"Please, Dad, let's go. Let's run." The lights bounced and turned with the road. "We know the mountain. They don't. Please Daddy, let's go."

He had slapped me. "Find Derrik. Do you remember what he looks like?"

"Yes."

"Be good. His wife might hate you, but she cares for him. Run!" He shoved me away and walked into the barn.

The two cars stopped. I ducked into the tall grass.

From the cars, six vampires clad in black flowing and old-fashioned clothing rushed into the barn. I didn't see Derrik among them, but they moved so fast.

One vampire raced toward me. I dashed across the field, but he was faster.

Xiao grabbed me by the shoulder.

"No, not you. I need to find Derrik Miller," I cried.

"Good," Xiao said, "because that's who I'm taking you to."

As if I were a princess in a gown, instead of a farm girl in overalls, Xiao held my arm. "Don't look at the violence, sweetheart. I can shield you from the pain."

"Please, can't you save my dad too?"

"Your dad?" Xiao wrapped his arm around my shoulder. "Let's get you to Derrik. Keep your eyes down. Don't look."

Bill screamed.

"Please Mr. Bai! Help him."

Xiao covered my eyes. He whispered something, but I didn't understand the language. Still whispering, he took off his coat and put it over my shoulders. (Later, I would learn Xiao dominated my mind, and Loretta dominated Derrik's, so we did not experience Bill's dismemberment.)

True to his word, Xiao opened the front door to the car where Derrik sat with a dour expression. I thought he really did look like an old-timey villain. I scooted across the bench seat toward him. "I'm Norma."

"We know." Derrik looked toward the barn. He wept (and would silently weep most of the way home.)

Xiao turned on the radio, made a U-turn and drove away. My last glimpse of the barn, I saw the fire.

"Don't look. I know it's hard." As he drove, Xiao changed the station quickly. "Hey, *The Shadow*! Do you like mysteries?"

S TARING AT THE BOXES, I PULLED THE BOX down with my name. It was the heaviest of all three boxes. Still I wondered.

Inside were neatly labeled files of old workbooks, themes, book and film reports, and sketches. Pascaline and Derrik encouraged me to learn a variety of subjects and use my years as an adolescent to become an "accomplished young lady." I hadn't expected Derrik to keep old school work. *Maybe all vampire parents keep mementos of their offspring.* Behind the school work sat two old baby food jars of earth labeled Widow Rollin's Farm and Barn. If I opened them, I would be overwhelmed with childhood memories. I kept them closed.

I sought the monthly reports about whether or not I was a true vampire and my temperament between November 1951 to June 1954.

Derrik, Pascaline, and Laurence claimed they witnessed only hints of William's gifts in my creativity, but none of the despondency that drove his insanity. Unless another vampire witnessed it, Derrik and Pascaline didn't mention my quarrelsome behavior. There were a few reports of possible sleepwalking or dayterrors, but only two reports of *Hysteria / Gross Stress Reactions* though I had suffered several episodes. The first report was of the time Charles scolded me for running in the hallway. Terrified, I screamed and ran into Derrik's apartment. I ultimately was sent to my room to think about what I had done.

The second report was about an episode that started as a contest of wills about turning off the radio and ended in a shouting match. Derrik called me an ingrate and I told him I hated him. Even before I started to panic, the argument was loud enough Loretta and her enthralled heard. There were other panic attacks, but Derrik and Pascaline researched treatment plans and guided me gently through the worst of it.

I flipped through other minor offenses--mostly arguments with Derrik or his thrall Mary about appropriate dinner dress--until I found my greatest act of disobedience.

Though Vampire Norma Mae Rollins made grave mistakes on 1952/04/08, she is not intentionally criminal. She is a confused fledgling, driven by vampire instincts, but unable to express her needs. Her creator did not explain the vampire need of earth, nor did I. I didn't believe it was possible for a vampire to need earth of a childhood home.

As reports 1951/11/18 through 1952/03/10 show: my descendant requested asked several times to see her birth mother and I forbade it. [Copies attached]

On the night in question, Norma woke before me and drank two pints of cow's blood in order not to harm her mother or any human. She left a note telling me she must see her mother. [Copy attached] There was no call to the Issaquah, Renton, or Seattle police which could be traced back to the car or to Norma. Widow Rollins is alive.

Logically, the only way the vampire could

accomplish gathering her earth before sunrise was the use of a car. Though Norma does not have a Washington State Driver's License, she had driven a tractor several times prior to her change. She returned the car, relinquished a week's pocket money to pay for gas, and washed it in the garage without instruction. I denied Norma her routine trip to the cinema which she accepted without quarrel. She is repentant for disobeying my direction and confused about why she had set out to see her mother but had gathered earth. She claimed Tiger Mountain told her what to do. Lady Pascaline and I discussed this in depth with Laurence Roch. We have come to believe she was acting upon vampire intuition as he did after he was changed.

I will not refute my descendant made a grave error in judgment, but as her guardian and mentor, I made the greater mistake. I refused to use my cognitive abilities to associate the requests with a commonly-known vampire need and not realizing that unlike other vampires, Norma is in deep mourning for the loss of her life. However, the claiming of earth shows that Norma is, without a doubt, a vampire.

Over the past months, Norma has been overwhelmingly obedient and good-natured to Lady Pascaline, Laurence Roch and myself. However, as a member of my bloodline and household, I am ultimately at fault for gaps in her education. I have set about to remedy that with an initiation manual as my guide on how to instruct her.

The addendum was the transcript of a short discussion which mainly were complaints about how Derrik and Pascaline spoiled me. The other vampires had grown up with "spare the rod" attitudes and felt a lecture and a missed trip to the cinema was not enough of a punishment.

Charles challenged my place in the coven.

Pascaline claimed I was a beloved child of God, because whether by accident or design, I had survived the initiation rite. Then she reminded them life and undeath were too complicated to exist with shame.

Loretta made a motion:

Norma is innocent due to her age, but this act of larceny will be held as evidence against her if she makes a similar mistake in the future and might count against her when she puts in her application for full membership into the coven in 1964.

8/0 in favor.

The report didn't help me with understanding coven justice. It only confirmed what I already knew. Derrik, with assistance from Pascaline and Laurence, protected me until I was able to protect myself.

Derrik purposely omitted several points from the report such as not only had I borrowed the car without permission, but I also skipped lessons and took a nightgown and jar of whitening powder from Pascaline. Most importantly, Derrik neglected to inform the other vampires, I had visited my mother.

I N 1952, THE I-90 BRIDGE AND HIGHWAY DID not span Lake Washington and make the trip to Issaquah a twenty minute affair. I drove around Lake Washington to Renton and followed a two-lane trucking route to my mother's farm under the shadow of Tiger Mountain. Careful to remain at the speed limit and watching for deer who might jump into the road, the trip took two hours one way.

I parked close to the farm on a paved road. I briefly thought about calling Derrik and telling him I made it to Issaquah but feared to worsen my mistake. The mountain spoke to me in the movement of the wind. It remembered me and all who played on her slopes. Wearing one of Pascaline's translucent white night gowns, I covered on my hands, face, and hair with streaks of whitening powder.

Trying to ignore the mountain's voice, I hurried to the farm. My first impression was it looked much more run-down than I remembered. Worse, my sheepdog, Barley, didn't recognize me and barked wildly, snapping at the end of his tether. I couldn't get into the house.

"Mom," I called.

The curtain was drawn back on the window. My mother came out on the porch with a hoe. She looked withered and careworn as if I had aged a decade in the nine months I had been gone. Abject misery filled her eyes.

"Mom." I held back the tears threatening to fall.

"Norma, is that you?"

"I'm sorry I snuck out with my friends, Mom."

My mother claimed that it didn't matter. "Come here. Come here so I can see you."

"I can't. I'm dead."

My mother fell to her knees.

To ease my mother's grief, I claimed, "I was hit by a truck, died instantly, and am now surrounded by angels who care for me." I begged my mother not to mourn then promised, "Heaven's a huge place so don't worry if we can't find each other right away. I love you, but I have to go."

I stepped away in the darkness. The mountain instructed me to claim earth from my mother's garden. I went around back and found two large pickle jars where my mother habitually left them. The first I filled with earth from my yard. Memories of childhood overwhelmed me. With the loam between my fingers, I could remember every detail.

Then the mountain whispered, "Find your second birthplace."

I found the old burnt barn where I was Reborn and

filled a second jar. Tears ran down my cheeks due to the good, bad, and horrific memories with Bill, yet I knew I must fill the jar. Not only for me, but for Derrik who still mourned. I searched for evidence Bill had died, but there was none.

On the drive to Seattle, I thought up excuses by the minute. At first, I was nervous about being punished. Then sad because Derrik trusted me, and I ruined it. Then, incensed because if he had only been reasonable, I would not have taken the car.

I was still angry when I saw Derrik and Pascaline in the garage. As I parked, I wanted to hurt them, before they hurt me. I opened the car door, ready to fling: "You're not my parents..."

Before I could say a word, Derrik explained in a firm voice: "If you want to borrow the car, you must ask first and earn your license."

While the report spoke of my confusion and repentance: the report didn't mention Derrik and Pascaline helped me wash off the country mud and the million bugs who met their end on the windshield. They carried my earth, packed it in small jars, and answered my questions. How when I started to cry, Pascaline held me until I calmed while Derrik lectured about the purpose of Washington State Driving Statutes. I also got a warning from Laurence about skipping my lessons, but he didn't punish me either.

As the report testified: Derrik did not allow me to go to the cinema that week, but it didn't say why. The thralls, Mary and Aldo, claimed they were furious at me for breaking coven statutes and human law which endangered Derrik.

In truth, Aldo was livid Bill was dead and Derrik wasn't the type of vampire he signed up to serve. Mary was livid at all the minor inconveniences she endured because her vampire had a young person in his life. They insisted I be punished or I would have faced something much worse from them. I heard them think about holding my hand in front of an open window. They didn't want to kill me, but they thought a good burn would teach me to behave like a vampire.

I hated the memories of my youth.

Chapter 10

6:30 PM

I FLOPPED AGAINST THE WALL AND PRESSED a palm to my face. I closed my eyes and drifted off, but jolted awake once I heard Derrik moving about the kitchen.

I scrambled to my feet and hoped he was in a better mood. Looking at the old files on the floor, I slipped them back into the boxes in perfect order.

Derrik melted a pat of butter into a frying pan. Bacon and eggs were on the counter beside him. Hugo was sitting at the table with a tired look in his eyes with his first latte of the day.

"I see you haven't slept. Are you hungry?" Derrik asked.

"Yes. I looked in your closet."

Derrik stiffened, but asked, "And what treasures did you find?"

"Did Bill survive his final death? Could he want vengeance?"

He grimaced and cracked an egg into the pan. "I don't see how, but we aren't to speak of the Paper Flower Consortium's shame, especially this early."

Rage bubbled up in my stomach. "I can't solve this crime without getting Bill out of my head."

"You don't need to solve it at all. Marion will

eventually," Hugo said.

"No, she won't. She'll find the first suspect guilty. She might be right; she might be wrong. If Loretta believes it too, all Loretta's children will vote with her. We don't have the numbers. Plenty of vampires would love it if the proof of the Paper Flower Consortium's shame no longer existed and Ryan is also in danger being behind in his dues."

"You ought not say such things about your coven siblings." Derrik scrapped the bottom of the pan too hard as he flipped Hugo's egg.

"Do you honestly think any of Loretta's children would cast blame on each other?"

Hugo's mouth opened wide; his eyes rested on Derrik.

"We didn't feel Bill's death. Loretta and Xiao ensured we wouldn't. Xiao got us out of there."

"Only because it was no place for a fourteen-year-old girl." Derrik set down Hugo's plate so hard on the table it clattered.

"Back off, Normie," Hugo said.

I ignored him. "And everyone left before sunrise. What if he survived?"

Derrik fried my eggs and covered them in blood just like I liked them and handed me the plate. By the time Derrik sat down with his own breakfast, Hugo had finished.

"You two have much to discuss." He went to shower and dress.

"I should have invested in tech companies," Derrik said softly. "But I remember all the money I lost in the Depression. The stock market is precarious black magic. I bought Treasury bills, but..." He sighed. He could afford an upper-middle-class lifestyle, but no more. He didn't want more.

"A vampire's life is one of shoulda, woulda, coulda. I used to wish I had mined bitcoin. But that bubble also went pop." I made an explosion gesture. "And will rise and fall again."

"So much volatility," Derrik said softly. "Still, I might've purchased a lovely little house on Mercer Island for Hugo. Make him happy. Keep him and Maria safe from all this. Keep you safe too."

"That's why I need information. I'm sorry I looked through your stuff without asking, but I refiled it carefully."

He laughed. "How well you know people. What do you want to know?"

I started with what I thought was an easy question. "Why'd you choose Bill as your Firstborn? Besides you were in love."

Derrik nodded. "Bill was charming, funny, and a delight to be with. Laurence and Bill's romance ended shortly after he joined the program. It was easy to fall in love with him. I ran his numbers against mine and saw our compatibility.

"Bill left his wife and bought a condominium. Pascaline was hurt, but she wanted me to be happy. She took her own lovers. Those early years were halcyon times for us. Everyone loved him. He was extremely intelligent and existed as very few did. I am sorry you never knew that aspect of his personality."

Derrik's normally perfect posture curled over half-eaten eggs. "Please, forgive me. I wronged you before you were born and reborn."

I squeezed his hand. "You've nothing to apologize for."

Derrik studied his eggs as if he expected them to add to the conversation. "I thought I knew Bill. I was arrogant in my abilities. In hindsight, your Rebirth or some other disaster seems inevitable after what I saw when I transformed him."

He withdrew his hand from mine and cracked his knuckles and rubbed the webbing in between. I did not interrupt. This was part of the information I was waiting for.

"In the moment of true connection, I witnessed the despondency he hid. Worse, I saw his sins.

"I briefly considered killing Bill, but I loved him. I finished the rite. I did my best to put it out of my head. Bill never abused me. He told me he would never touch a woman again. And what he had with Aldo...well, that was consensual. For years after, he was a joy. He left his job at Boeing and designed the new main building with the newest technologies and room for the coven to grow. He created a legacy that no sin can erase.

"Slowly the melancholy returned. He disappeared for the summer months so he could hunt beasts and humans. After his younger son died in Korea, he grew beyond paranoid. Miserable. Then he left and..." Derrik voice hitched. "I felt your rebirth. Agata barely felt it, but Jakub did."

"At first, I hated him. Then I told myself when winter lengthened the nights, Bill would arrive with another vampire, who would be untrained, but consented to vampirism. I even hoped it was a woman. I had a vampire wife so would he, but we would be together.

"I went to him and saw you, running with deer and catching rabbits with your bare hands." He couldn't look up at my face. I felt his rage, not directed at me as I am now, but at the memory.

"You wanted to kill me?" I asked though it was not a question.

"I thought about ripping out your throat and chaining you to a tree and bringing Bill home. But he mourned his human son, and his mind was filled with love for you, and there were dozens of bodies rotting away..."

"You still love him?"

"Vampires love all their creations."

I didn't want to disillusion him. "I suppose they do."

Derrik must have heard my thought because he took my hands in his. "Bill loved you. As furious as I was, he asked me to take you to the coven and keep you safe or stay with you there and be your father too. But you were not safe with only him."

"He could be cruel to his human children, but to appease my conscience, I told him the coven would kill you. I left you there.

"A few weeks later, a month? At any rate, he called and asked once more. He told me what happened between you. I told myself he was exaggerating. I believed he had punished you to be sure, but it couldn't possibly be as bad as he claimed. Jakub overheard the conversation. I would have given anything to have him back. I would have told myself ... the others anything.

"His last act of sanity was to come to the meeting. His last words to me were, 'I have to get her away from me before I sink deeper into the sun.' I told him to run. He did not."

"You believe he was happy to end his existence?" I asked.

"I don't know, but he feared time more than the coven's justice. Pascaline said he laughed when they came for him. That is why I believe Bill has met Final Death."

I took a deep breath. That wasn't what the report said, but I already knew the reports didn't say everything.

Derrik cracked his knuckles again.

"Whatever you did or didn't do, you made up for it all the years I resided here. I wasn't the easiest kid, but you kept me anyway. And I might've only had a limited understanding of the coven when I arrived, but I knew keeping me hurt your reputation and still does."

"The only thing I would have done differently is taken you away from Bill sooner. You brightened my existence. All of our existences."

"If the coven was stationary, the elder vampires would have forgiven my lineage. Now every initiate in the program hears about the crimes of the Vampire William T. Caruso."

"Only as a warning that eternity can drive a vampire insane."

"You call me the beloved mistake of your Firstborn, which I suppose is better than the Shame of the Paper Flower Consortium, but it still hurts every time you say it."

"There is no way else to speak of the truth. Everyone must know you are my descendant and not some wild foundling who subsisted on my charity." Derrik sighed. "Even now, I fear for you. You are right about that. I wish Pascaline would wake up."

"Me too."

"My eggs are cold." Derrik picked up his plate and scraped his breakfast into the compost bin. "Excuse me."

Watching him leave the kitchen, I regretted the conversation. This knowledge didn't get me any closer to solving the crime. All I did was dredge up painful memories, destroy Derrik's appetite, and my own eggs had also gotten cold.

Since no one was there to be appalled by bad manners, I gobbled them in as few bites as possible and let them slip down my throat.

Then I washed and dried the dishes. I opened the cupboard. Its arrangement was the same as I remembered, so I put away the dishes.

Legends tell of the danger of inviting a vampire in one's home, which is a shame because no matter what people believe, vampires always try to be excellent house guests.

Chapter 11

8 PM

I KNOCKED ON THE DOOR OF THE PAPER Flower Consortium's IT department. Summer looked up from her three monitors on an L-shaped desk and gestured for me to enter. The room was set up for two workers. Over the desks was a gray wall of strange artifacts, taxidermy, and skeletons. Xiao's empty chair made the office all the more depressing.

Summer appeared to be the perfect vampire's thrall. Her smooth brown throat was covered in a tall velvet choker. She wore a silky black slip and with a gothy-ribbon corset bustier edged in purple. Her dark eyeshadow was a bit smudged in a fashionable way. "You look really tired. One of your day terrors?" Summer sounded concerned, or I hoped I heard concern.

"Just trouble sleeping. Sorry to bother you, but is it possible to find out if a stranger's phone was used at the Fellowship?"

Summer smiled. "Norms, are you playing detective?"

I didn't like the word 'playing,' but it didn't matter. "Yes."

"How can I help?"

"Can I ask you some questions?"

"Sure."

"Really?" I wrote *Summer* in my pad.

"Whatever happens in the coven stays in the coven. It's not like everybody doesn't already know everybody's business," Summer said.

"Are you happy here?"

"Yes."

"With Jakub?"

"A man learns a lot in five hundred years. He's interesting."

I drew a smiley face.

"Do you have any problems with Xiao?"

"Nope. He's respectful to me both as a co-worker and as a lady of the coven."

I wrote X and drew another smiley face.

"I heard Fern might be having an affair. Is that true?"

Summer laughed. "I don't know if it's true. Xiao might just be a jealous vampire. He's been complaining about how Fern has bite marks he knows he didn't give her."

"What does Fern say?"

Summer patted my leg. "She's been looking around for some time. Xiao is good looking and he tries to please her, but they aren't compatible if you know what I mean, but then I suppose you don't."

But I did.

"I went to college — U-Dub class of 1958. I became a master of disguise so I could date. And I still go to vampire-friendly clubs to meet people."

"Really? It's too bad that's not common knowledge. More people would like you if you seemed more like the other vampires."

"Derrik and Pascaline know."

"Lady Pascaline was asleep before I joined The Paper Flower Consortium and Derrik doesn't speak openly about such things."

"Well, if you had been at Sunday Morning Dinner, you could've enjoyed his routine complaints that I'm going to clubs when I ought to settle down with a thrall and attend church each Sabbath."

Summer laughed again.

I brought my questions back to the point. "Any idea who Fern would be with?"

"If I had to take a guess: I'd say Ryan or maybe even Marion. She smiles when one of them walks into the room."

"Everybody does. Hey, did you see that young man with Ethan?"

"White kid sweating under tweed," Summer said.

"He was on his phone a few times during the Sabbath. And I got his name: Gavin Sean Tupper. I wondered if he was doing something Xiao didn't like which is why there was a fight."

Summer brightened. "What a great idea! We generally have less activity during the Sabbath so if he was doing something hinky, we can find out. I'll show you."

Summer woke her computer and opened a window which showed the network activity. She typed in the date and time. She clicked on a link which brought up a list.

I scanned over Summer's shoulder. I saw iPhones, iPads, Androids, desktops — most designated by the given names of vampires or thralls she recognized.

"Look at this." Summer pointed to an IP number. "This phone was streaming something to YouTube during the Sabbath...."

I suddenly thought of Ivy on the beach with her phone taking videos of Samuel. "If he was live-streaming in a coven, I bet a million bucks he's trying to film vampires."

"Let's see what we can find." She opened her browser and typed "Live-streaming from a vampire Sabbath."

A video showed Gavin whispering into his phone from the temple bathroom.

"Hello, my friends," he said. "Gavin, here, I'm live from a real vampire Sabbath for my entry in the Proof of

Supernatural Challenge. While this looks like a standard bathroom, it's part of a vampire temple."

He pointed the phone at the wall of stalls.

"A vampire might have pee'd in this very spot. Yes, I have it on good authority that vampires do urinate!"

Watching Gavin take a sample of the toilet water in a tiny vial, Summer and I started laughing

"Remember the magic is all around us and I'm going to prove it!"

Ethan came into the bathroom. "Put that away, boy."

Gavin's voice sounded hard. "Don't call me boy."

The phone went dark for a few minutes, but we could hear footsteps, voices, and see the flickering of lights as the two moved through the coven.

"Ick, he didn't wash his hands," Summer said. "While we're waiting, grab that laptop and see what the Proof of Supernatural Challenge is."

I quickly found the next video. Three YouTube stars popped up on the screen laughing. All three looked to be in their thirties. One of the women had big hair and a 1980's look. There was Gavin and the third was Ivy.

"Oh, no."

"What?"

I pointed at the monitor. "This lady. Ivy. I pulled her out of Golden Gardens on the Sabbath. She was pestering one of Poseidonsons."

"She's going by Ivy?" Summer asked.

"That's not her name?"

"You don't know her?"

"I knew she looked familiar, but no I don't."

"Derrik is right to complain about you never coming home. That's Irene: Ryan's Irene," Summer said.

"We've got to look at her other videos."

Irene/Ivy claimed to be an experienced ghost hunter. In her introductory video, she declared, "I know the supernatural exists, because I spent seven years possessed by a demon."

"I doubt Ryan's going to like being called a demon. Do you think this will make the Consortium angry?" I whispered.

"Why are you whispering," Summer whispered back.

I shrugged. "I don't know."

In her normal tone, Summer said, "I doubt Ryan will like it and I doubt the Consortium will care. Notice how carefully she's not mentioning vampires."

The screen with Gavin's video popped back on.

I turned toward the suddenly-lit screen. "He's in the Sanctum!"

"I am about to film a sleeping vampire." Gavin passed the efficiency apartment and went into the darkness with a bright light. He recorded Pascaline's glass coffin. Since vampires did not cast a reflection, cameras also couldn't pick them up. It was dim, but I could just barely see Pascaline's black gown against the coffin's black satin.

"Ethan let him into the Sanctum?" I asked.

"I can't believe that. A thrall would never do that to the vampire they loved. The kid probably followed him," Summer said.

More voices filled the video. Gavin shoved his phone in his pocket. Then he was in the temple. In the pews ahead of him were Kuma and Summer chatting, but the gowns of Agatha, Kanae and Hitomi moved past them. All the camera saw was their clothing and hair ornaments.

"We all look like invisible people. The enthralled are the only ones showing up. You look so beautiful, Summer."

"Ah, bless you."

"At least, most of the comments don't think it's real," I said. Most talked about how they saw better special effects in the 1940's *The Invisible Man*.

I studied the Proof Challenge Playlist. Each one posted a pre-challenge video. The girl with big hair hunted werewolves. Irene/Ivy searched for a sea monster. Gavin sought vampires in Georgetown. He even showed the front of the Paper Flower Consortium.

I shook my head. "This is going to be a big clean up. I better tell Agata and Jakub. And tell Ryan about Irene."

"And Marion."

"And Marion," I repeated, but not wanting to talk to that honored sister.

"What about the girl who wants to record werewolves?"

"I'll call to the HOA president to know to keep an eye out, but if she's stupid enough to enter their congregation without a good reason, well that problem will likely work itself out. The werewolves would probably just have a barbecue."

July 29, 2019

Chapter 12

Midnight

AS I ENTERED THE CLINIC, AGATA SMILED. However, dark circles had developed under her eyes and her normally smooth skin, sagged somehow.

Xiao was in bed. His eye was still milky, but patches of skin were growing back. An IV drip was in his arm. Loretta's youngest, Tabitha Jones (no human relation to Ryan), had donated her blood. Four of her sisters under Loretta giggled amongst themselves in the corner, their left wrists bandaged. They had also been contributing blood for Xiao. It was good vampires could use any blood type.

"I need to talk to you, Bunică."

"Norma, my dear one, I don't want you giving blood. You don't weigh enough."

I felt so alone. I wished Agata would allow me to donate blood. Tabitha and Mi-Yeong were petite and slender; I was as tall as Mi-Yeong. I probably didn't weigh much less than them, but for the younger vampires Agata used the same requirement the humans did: 110 pounds.

"I've been looking around, and I found some things."

"Tell Marion."

"I will." *I must think logically.* I still didn't know who staked Xiao. I didn't even recognize Irene. If it weren't for Summer, I wouldn't even know about the Proof of the Supernatural Challenge. "I just wanted to check to see how things are going here."

"Feeling any better, Xiao?"

He shook his head.

"I'm sorry for your pain. I wish I could take it away."

He gave me a thumbs up.

I thought about the position of the stake. Whoever came at him came at him fast. The window had to be broken first — which made sense with what he said he saw. I didn't have the strength to stake him— or at least I didn't think I did. Maybe if I snuck up behind him, but not a frontal attack. Loretta's daughters probably couldn't have done it either. Though Michella and Vera had the leverage of their greater height, their vampire powers were only decades matured. It had to be someone physically stronger. Or more than one person?

Agata bandaged Tabitha's wrist.

Loretta's five daughters giggled again. It seemed strange to laugh, but even vampires were known to laugh when stressed and find comfort in their peers. They had different skin tones, hair, and eye color. Yet, they were interchangeable in their black silk blouses and tailored slacks. It was almost a uniform. I hated myself for thinking that. It made me a bad detective and a worse fixer.

I studied each one: Vera was Black. Michella, Tabitha, and Jessica were white. Mi-Yeong was of Korean descent. I studied their blouses. Vera wore a pretty lace top, but not a thread was out of place. Michella had a Peter Pan collar. The other three ladies' blouses had triangle shaped lapels. Four wore their hair a few inches below their shoulders. Vera sported a natural Afro style split into two ponytails.

Their fingers were soft and perfectly manicured. I hadn't had a manicure in years. *Maybe Derrik would want to get a mani-pedi with me. That's something we both like to do.*

I considered their jobs. Michella, Vera, and Jessica all

worked for Jakub. Michella processed the mortgages, home equity and car loans for coven members. Vera and Jessica were accountants. Mi-Yeong and Tabitha ran a custom clothing shop which employed a few thralls and serviced the coven, Seattle's werewolf, goth, and cosplay communities.

"Normie, dear, are you still playing detective?" The eldest, Michella, asked.

"Yes."

"Did you want to question us?" she said.

"You'll let me?"

The ladies surrounded me.

"Any suspects?" Jessica whispered.

Another twittering of nervous giggles. *Was I ever that young?* "Maybe we should go to my office so Xiao can sleep."

They all agreed. Vera took my arm as we walked. The women led me into my office. They squished together on my leather sofa. I rolled my desk chair so I might look at their fluttering hands, too-high voices, wide-eyed expressions on their pretty faces, the bloody tears of sweat. They didn't want to upset Marion by helping me, but they wanted to be safe again.

That's why they became vampires in the first place. A modern vampire's life was one of security and a quiet life. They all loved their jobs, each other, and their maker who was a mix of mentor/mother/cool big sister all rolled into one. Loretta accepted them and gave them a family who never hurt each other and a warm, safe place to reside, but they remembered their former lives. They did not want to go back. I could understand that. Though I had mourned my life with my mother, I would never want to go back to Bill.

I took out my phone and asked if I might record their voices.

"Oh, yes, you should," Vera said. Her sisters all nodded.

I asked where they were when Xiao was staked.

Tabitha and Mi-Yeong were enjoying their thralls and

Michella, was having a romantic encounter with Marcus Smith of the Bellevue coven. Vera and Jessica were sleeping in their coffins but were awoken by Derrik and Loretta screaming at the stairwell.

"I thought Marcus left with the others." I asked.

Michella blushed. "No, he left about 4 am with Roger. Roger brought his own car."

"Marcus was with you during the unfortunate event?"

"Yes."

"Did you ever leave Marcus alone?"

"I went to the bathroom after..." She lowered her voice. "Do you know about such things?"

Since my response worked with Summer, I answered the same way in a deadpan voice. "Yes. I went to college."

"But that was in the 50s."

"Plenty of young people in the 50s were happy for my affections. Things were more closeted, but people did the same things they've always done. Where do you think baby boomers came from?"

The ladies nodded.

Michella spoke in her natural voice again. "When I came out, he went to wash up, but I don't think he went anywhere when I was bathing. I would've heard. Then we went to see what happened together. You were so brave."

Keeping the women talking and comfortable, I smiled and said, "Thanks. Derrik said I'm too reckless."

"Two sides of the same coin, I'd think," Jessica said.

Her sisters agreed.

"And your understanding is Roger was with Marion?"

"Yes."

"But you didn't see it."

"Sure, but where else would he be?" Jessica said. "We don't have first-hand knowledge, of course, but Marion's always pretty happy after Roger visits."

"If I showed you some lace, would you know who wore

it?"

I pulled out the baggie of lace I fished from the garbage and handed it to Mi-Yeong first who held it by the plastic before passing it to her coven sister. "It's machine-made, so not a coven vampire."

"Maybe a thrall or initiate would wear something like that," Tabitha added.

"If you had a chunk of lace ripped from your gown what would you do?"

"I would toss the garment into the donation bin," Mi-Yeong said. "Unless the fabric was expensive then I would remake it into something else. But this is not expensive."

Tabitha nodded. "It's too cheap to be added as trim to anything Mi-Yeong and I make, it'd ruin the look."

"Thanks. The donation bin will be my next stop."

For the first time in my undeath, I listened to the younger vampires. I held Mi-Yeong's perfect hand who sat closest. I passed around tissues. They were scared. It was hard to focus on work. They wanted to do something, so they gave their honorable brother blood.

I said softly, "Don't be scared. I promised Derrik. I'll not leave until Marion or I can figure out who staked Xiao and I promise you all too."

"Aren't you frightened?"

"Terrified."

"You don't show it, Normie."

"I am. I couldn't sleep during the day and was so frightened at breakfast, I upset Derrik with some stupid questions."

They all looked at each other. "Can we ask you a question?"

"Sure."

"Is it true you've worked for..." Vera made a brief pause and whispered: "werewolves?"

"Yeah. What's the big deal? Derrik and Jakub work for

werewolf clients."

"But that's here in the coven, not in the world. How do you know they'll not bite you?" Vera asked.

"They have similar initiation requirements as vampires. I'm more likely to be killed than bitten."

They looked even more nervous. "How do you know you won't be killed?"

"Quality customer service protects me." I paused. "Being part of this coven protects me. Not only is the Paper Flower Consortium powerful in terms of reputation, but Derrik wouldn't help werewolves with legal services who hurt a coven member.

"Oh, and funny t-shirts. Werewolves love puns."

"We often wonder why you don't dress like a vampire especially with a maker's maker like Derrik," Michella said.

"My work can be pretty dirty. Just the other night, I had to help a merman at Golden Gardens. It's why I was late for the Sabbath. I had to shower, or I'd have smelled like algae. But I dressed in the skirt. That's like a vampire, isn't it?"

"Of course. The next time everyone saw you, you were in..." Tabitha made a dramatic pause. "...shorts with cats on them. And now ripped jeans."

"Oh. Well, I was warm when I went to my coffinroom. I can't wait until we replace the old air conditioner."

"Why don't you sleep in silk?"

I didn't know how to explain my feeling about different fabrics. "I don't know, but the jeans help me to feel like I'm working like...."

"Like armor!" Vera said.

"Yes! Exactly," I said. "Hey, can you help me with something else?"

The ladies seemed interested in helping so I pulled out my phone and brought up the picture of Ivy. "Is this Ryan's Irene?"

They all agreed it was. After they watched the video, Jessica told her: "I can't believe Irene would be so cruel. Well, maybe I can. It was pretty bitter."

"Will you tell me about it?"

"Well, Ryan..." Vera trailed off.

"Ryan, Derrik, and Hugo told me Irene left because she wanted a life, but I hoped to get your point of view."

"Three years ago, Ryan had a paper not published. Then he didn't get a grant. A few of his former human colleagues died. He couldn't find anyone who wanted to work with him due to his schedule. Irene and Ryan started to fight over little things. They never made up. It got bigger. They both said emotionally abusive things. He was lazy, useless. She was manipulative and spent too much money.

"She started to hit him," Mi-Yeong added. "I don't think any of us really understood how abusive it had gotten because he was so ashamed."

"She asked for her severance and left," Jessica said.

"You better check with Jakub about Irene's Non-disclosure Agreement," Michella said.

"Yes, I will. I want to show Marion this too, but I don't know how to approach her the right way."

Vera smiled. "You tend to jump into situations. She takes a longer view in the way vampires do when they are over thirty when transformed."

I left my office, smiling. This was the longest conversation I ever had with any of Loretta's children. Maybe Summer was right. If I seemed to be the normal vampire, maybe they'd like me better.

Agata and Derrik were always trying to make me seem normal. Everyone wanted what's best for me. It was time I made the effort. Maybe I'd even get some new vampire clothes from Mi-Yeong and Tabitha's shop, but first to the donation bin.

☾HE DONATION BIN WAS FILLED WITH SPLIT leather pants, damaged lace, silks, and blood-stained socks. King County accepted ripped clothing for recycling to keep clothes out of the landfills. The coven kept a donation bin. Twice a year, Cam tossed everything in the laundry and brought undamaged clothing to charity, the rest to the recycling program. Nothing looked like it was missing lace trim and the lace pieces were mostly intact.

I closed my eyes. Whatever the murderer was wearing while staking Xiao would most likely be covered in blood. Maybe it would be thrown away rather than in the donation bin. Or maybe it was sitting in someone's sink, but I wouldn't be able to search the apartments without Marion or one of the elders. Pascaline might help if she was not in torpor, but Derrik would never do anything like search another vampire's home. I dare not ask the other elders.

I DECIDED TO TRY UTMOST POLITENESS.
"I must speak with you, my honorable sister," I said to Marion. "I asked our honorable sisters under Loretta about the lace, and they thought it looked machine made."

"What does that mean?" Marion scraped her palm over her face to hide her frustration

"A vampire wouldn't wear it."

"Yes, I already knew that." She spoke through her teeth. "Which is why I threw it in the trash. I asked you to remain out of this. Why don't you go save a werewolf or whatever the hell you do?"

"My honorable sister, I'm visiting Derrik, and I keep an office. I have every right to be here."

"I am aware."

I knew I was heading in the wrong direction. "Have you looked into the young man who was here?"

"Yes. Summer sent me the links of the videos already as you requested and I interviewed Ethan."

I wondered if I should tell her Ethan originally lied to me about who the young man was, but maybe it didn't matter. "Yeah. Ethan told me Gavin tried to take a picture of Xiao and Fern."

"Ethan said Gavin left after the fight."

"But I heard voices on the stairs last night. They sounded pretty angry."

"And this was when?"

"After Xiao was staked. See, I was getting blood splatter pictures. I'll show you..."

"My honored sister, while you are old in years, you are also naive. Voices carry in the stairwells. Everyone is upset. If you aren't leaving, you ought to remain with Derrik or our sisters," Marion said. "If you actually believe someone who is here who shouldn't be, then it's too dangerous to be running around alone."

"Can I email you my blood splatter pictures?" I brought up a picture and showed her. "See, I tried to get the measurements."

Marion's expression became pinched. "Very well."

Chapter 13

1 AM

TRYING TO DECIDE MY NEXT STEP, I PACED the second-floor hallway. The corridor was empty except a single enthralled human with a blonde, shoulder-length bob that bounced with her steps. I knew she was Vera's thrall, but couldn't remember her name, so I just said, "Good evening."

"Good evening, Norma." The woman's voice was falsely high and demure as she replied and stepped aside. It reminded me of a little girl voice — which I hated. I walked past, turned the corner to find a quiet place to think.

Behind me, the woman screamed.

I darted back to the scream. The woman stood alone, clutching the door jam.

"What's wrong?"

"No. No..."

"What did you see?"

"A man. Someone who didn't belong here."

"Which way did he go?"

She pointed. "Lady Pascaline's."

I dashed down the hallway to Pascaline's apartment. I turned the doorknob. It was locked. I opened the door to Pascaline's apartment with my own key. I winced at the whiny hinges on the front door. I certainly wasn't able to sneak in.

Lemon cleaning solution filled my nostrils. Woven

heavy-grade polyethylene dust cloths covered the furniture. Ethan kept it tidy. It was empty, but observable shoe prints broke up the lines in the freshly vacuumed carpet.

I followed the prints to Pascaline's coffinroom and peeked through the open door. Gavin stood behind a tripod holding a camera.

I hid behind my beloved coven sister's antique dressing screen and watched as he slowly opened the coffin with fishing line. Then he slammed the lid shut as if it weren't empty. He did this three times.

Even shows on YouTube have scripts.

He went back into the living room, opened his laptop and imported the video.

I followed. "Hey."

He glanced over his shoulder and ran down the hall. He turned down the stairwell.

"Wait. I won't hurt you, but what are you doing here?"

At the bottom of the landing, he spun around a metal cross in one hand and his cellphone in the other. The shiny gray surface sparkled in the dim light.

"What are you doing?" I hoped that cross wasn't real silver.

"Back, back. Child vampires are an abomination."

"Okay. Someone's read too much *Interview with a Vampire*, or maybe not enough. Besides I am not a child, I was changed as a teenager."

Gavin hit me in the face with the cross. More surprised than hurt, I fell. It wasn't silver, just stainless steel. I covered my stinging cheek with my hand. "Owww. Why'd you do that?"

Holding his phone aloft, making sure he and I were in the frame, he shouted: "Look. The vampire child burns from the power of the Holy Cross!"

"It doesn't burn, you idiot. You smacked me in the face."

"Shut up, demon!" He pressed the cross onto my forehead. The crucifix's pointy bits scratched my brow. I wondered if somehow Gavin figured out a way to film vampires. I hoped not. I didn't want to be on YouTube.

"Stop it!" I kneed him in the groin.

He grunted and rolled off me, dropping his cross and phone.

I heard footsteps above me.

Bernie's voice rang out. "Get out of here, Gavin. You heard what Ethan said."

Gavin clambered to his feet. He grabbed for his phone but left the cross on the landing. He started down the steps. "The vampires are going to kill you!" Gavin shouted.

I wasn't sure if he was talking to me or Bernie.

"Delete that video!" I shouted back.

Bernie put his arm over my shoulder and swiped imaginary dust from my clothing. He clenched his fingers into my shoulder and faced me upward. "You better go to Derrik's. I'll take care of that boy."

"He was in Pascaline's apartment!"

"And what were you doing in Pascaline's apartment?"

"I was going to have a bath and take a lie down," I lied. "I have my own key."

"It's best if you go to Derrik's apartment now." Bernie ran down the stairs following Gavin.

"But..."

"I'll take care of everything, Norma."

"Make sure he deletes the video."

"I will."

IGNORING BERNIE'S DIRECTION, I WENT TO find Derrik. My forehead pulsed in pain where Jesus's bent knee had dug in. My arms weighed a million pounds. I peeked into Derrik's office through the door's glazing. He was alone at his desk, typing on his computer. I knocked on the door and entered in one movement.

"What in the world happened to your face?" he asked.

"Gavin — the man who came to the Sabbath — was in Pascaline's apartment. And he hit me with his cross. I'm thinking Xiao might've been right to attack him in the Fellowship."

"Violence is never correct." Derrik saved the file he was working on and stood up. "What did Ethan do when his guest hit you with the cross?"

"He wasn't there. Bernie said he was going to take care of him. Get him out."

"Then there's nothing to worry about." Derrik really was a terrible liar.

"But what if he's the one who staked Xiao?"

"Ethan is a trusted enthralled, it would not be him."

"No, I mean Gavin."

"Has Ethan ever shown himself to be untrustworthy?"

"No."

"You must give him and his guest the benefit of the doubt, my lamb. I can give you my blood to get that mark off your face." Derrik put the papers on his desk in a file which he placed in a file cabinet. Every movement was thoughtful. My ancestor was the perfect vampire. Michella, Vera, Jessica, Mi-Yeong, Tabitha were all perfect. And I was not. In a fleeting moment, I wondered if Derrik would really miss me if I met my final death. Or if even a little part of him would be relieved.

"You gave Xiao blood less than a day ago. Plus, it makes me look tough."

He tugged at his ear. "Indeed. You look like a battle-hardened warrior, but must you wear ripped trousers?"

"All teenagers wear ripped jeans. I split the knee at work, but some people even buy them pre-ripped," I said.

"What a strange time! Is the point to look impoverished,

so you don't get robbed?"

"I honestly have no idea." I wondered if I should tell him people were wearing ripped jeans before even Ryan's time. I decided against it. Derrik existed in a world where respectable people didn't wear torn clothing.

"If you won't take my blood, let's go home for lunch. You shouldn't be running around hungry."

"That man, Gavin, called me an abomination."

Derrik's mouth twisted into a grim frown, but he patted my shoulder. "What a rude fellow."

"He's right."

"What if he is? It changes nothing between us."

I appreciated he didn't deny it. I knew what I was. Most of the time, it didn't bother me, but as I had started to hope like I might fit in if I had dressed like a vampire, the words affected me more than expected.

"You are, and for eternity will be, my lamb."

"I spoke to my honored sisters under Loretta today," I said softly. "I felt friendly with them."

"Of course. You are the one who puts up the barriers, not they," Derrik opened the stairwell door for me.

I nodded. "They're scared. I don't think I ever understood how many people became vampires due to, for lack of a better word, lifestyle."

"The lifestyle?"

"The security part of it. I don't feel it, but the others do. Or did. Even Marion, though she won't admit it. Will you come with me to talk to her before lunch?"

Derrik held my arm, the same gentle way he held my arm when I was a girl. I might not feel the security of the coven, but I enjoyed the security in knowing I could always rely upon him.

"Good Evening, Marion," he said in his cool, calm way.

"Good Evening, Derrik ... and Norma," Marion replied with a thin-lipped smile.

"As you can see, my offspring was attacked by a man who is thought to be gone," Derrik pushed my hair back from my brow to show the scratch.

"Attacked?" She straightened in her chair.

"Gavin's still here. Or at least he was. He hit me in the face with a cross." I tried to mimic Derrik's cool calm vampire way. "He thought it would burn me."

"Are you saying a trusted thrall lied?" Marion asked.

"I don't know if Ethan knew. Gavin was hiding in Pascaline's coffinroom, and I think making a movie? Ethan's been spending a lot of the time in the Sanctum," I said. "He thinks Pascaline will be waking soon. But Bernie chased Gavin away."

"Very well. When Keith arrives in the morning, I'll question Ethan again and Bernie," Marion said.

"Thank you, our honored sister," Derrik said.

As we walked toward the stairwell, Derrik pulled out his pocket watch. "I am meeting a client in an hour, I'll start lunch, but would you be a dear and start a load of towels?" He sighed. "I hope Marion can solve this before Maria's moving day. Hugo won't want her to live here if he doesn't think it's safe."

"Don't worry. I will keep detecting."

"But you'll do the laundry first?"

"Of course."

Chapter 14

3 AM

I CIRCLED THE THREE COVEN BUILDINGS. Most of it looked like it normally did. The broken window had been boarded up. It seemed too high for it to be accidental. It must have been broken from inside.

Whoa. That has to be a clue. I rechecked my blood splatter photos. There was no glass! I looked under the window, no large amount of glass glittered on the pavement either. Someone must have cleaned it up, but why clean up the glass and leave the blood. It didn't make sense.

I moved toward the alley where the dumpsters were kept. The stench of weed lessened my ability to use my nose.

I detected someone following me in the light of the half moon. They moved too fast and silent to be human. I couldn't tell if it was one of the coven vampires, werewolf or something else. Perhaps I imagined it. I put my back against the nearest wall. The century-standing brick felt deep-rooted and secure, but I wondered if I had angered Marion enough that Marion would decide another vampire should be staked.

A silhouette in a black flowing gown moved through a street lamp: Loretta. What was she doing? Something sparkled, caught the next streetlight and flashed.

I hoped Loretta didn't blame me for Xiao's injury. If she did, my undeath would be over shortly.

"Lady Loretta." I bowed my head.

The elder vampire inclined her head in return. A thick band covered most of Loretta strawberry-blond braids. It was decorated with ostrich feathers, and a spiraling rhinestone pattern over her left ear sparkled in the streetlight. Her outfit didn't exactly blend in, but I doubted Loretta even owned a pair of slacks, much less jeans.

"Normie. I heard my daughters call you this name, you like it?"

"Yes, I do."

"Good." Loretta cupped my face and brushed a wayward curl from my brow. "Oh dear, are you not sleeping again? You must sleep if you wish to heal."

"Yes, honorable sister. It's hard in the coven, especially since everyone is so angry and frightened. I feel all of it in my brain."

"You always have been gifted, more so than even Derrik. Your natural gifts are why I've believed that William chose you among the children playing in the dark."

"But..."

"Normie dear, William was a known hedonist and liar. Whatever he said, whatever he did, he created his reasons for it as he went along. His lies went so thick not even he knew the truth. It is why he was able to trick Derrik."

I frowned.

"That sounds like I blame Derrik for his creation, but William fooled us all."

"Why do you look at me and see shame?"

"Because he shamed us. You must learn to exist with that truth."

"Yes, my honored sister. You are right. I owe..."

Loretta waved her hand. "Please, none of that nonsense that you say to other vampires. I know you too well. You pay what you owe to the coven in your dues. Pascaline and Derrik chose to keep you, to educate you as if they were their own child. You brought my sister happiness. I will always be grateful."

"What are you doing here?"

"I'm here to help you solve the mystery of who attacked my son. I brought this." She pulled a magnifying glass from her sparkling clutch.

Someone must have watched a Sherlock Holmes movie. I thought, but didn't say. Loretta couldn't read minds, her gifts were of a more persuasive nature, but I had to keep thoughts in check so an unpleasant word would not slip from my tongue.

"I swear it wasn't Carlos or me."

"You ought not swear in casual conversation," Loretta said. "I am surprised my honorable brother and sister did not teach you better. Or did you learn such things from the rogue? Pascaline shouldn't have gone in with that one. Noble born or not."

"Derrik, Laurence, and Pascaline often think I should not spend so much time mimicking humanity. I frighten them." *As much as I frighten you and Charles,* I thought but didn't say. I changed the subject. "Is Xiao doing any better?"

"Agata tells me it will be a long recovery period with much-needed blood."

"I'm sorry she will not allow me to donate."

"Agata has her reasons for everything. I was told I must be careful not to donate too much as I am also a few pounds lighter than the current requirements. Perhaps, the would-be killer would donate his."

"Or hers. Or theirs," I said. "We have to keep our minds open to all possibilities. Modern English is moving toward theirs for singular use when we don't know the gender."

Loretta linked her arm into mine. "How interesting! I always learn new things as I walk beside you. I hope we find the murderer so I might kill *them* and bequeath *their* blood to my son."

"Marion wants me to stop snooping."

"Of course. Marion wants to solve the crime. She is working on it, but she's also busy guarding the coven. You, on the other hand, have the gift of time and experience. My daughters tell me you interviewed them, but also asked their opinions and shared clues." She sighed. "If you and Marion both weren't so hardheaded perhaps you could act as buddy cops. I have seen many films. Buddy cops are how crimes are solved. You have a buddy, but he is but a shade and you sent him away ... very foolish...

"Pray, what's that awful smell?"

"Weed. Marijuana. Humans smoke it," I said.

"Hmm, pipeweed smells much nicer."

"Not all smell like this, it's a particularly skunky blend," I said.

"Do we have any clues yet?"

"I have a few. The first one we need to find out is about this man." I pulled out my phone. I tapped on the video she saved and handed the phone to Loretta.

"Ah, the young man from the Sabbath."

"He smacked me in the face."

I showed Loretta the lace. "Marion said I ruined the clue, so she threw it in the trash, but I keep thinking it will tell me something."

She examined the lace with her magnifying glass. "It's not high enough quality for my daughters or I to wear. Machine made."

"Mi-Yeong and Tabitha told me that too. They said a vampire wouldn't wear it, so I wondered if it was something Fern, Irene, or one of the other thralls might wear."

"It's more likely from a handkerchief."

"Handkerchief?" I asked disappointed. Another item found by the hundreds, perhaps thousands in the coven.

I showed Loretta the pictures of blood splatter and the video of Gavin in the coven bathroom.

"What is this?"

"YouTube. People make their own movies and shows on it."

"People make their own shows?"

"Yes. Camera equipment is much less expensive than it used to be — and there's no film."

"No film? How droll!"

The sound of traffic rumbling past on the nearby streets was pierced by a happy, uplifting song. No one answered the cell phone. We turned toward the noise, and Loretta suddenly stopped and sniffed the air. "Do you smell that?"

"I just smell the weed."

"Something is dead. Come, my dear."

With her eyeglass toward the ground, Loretta hurried down an alley. Rats scurried out of her way.

As I caught up to the elder, I smelled it too. Then saw the body. Irene was lying in a pile of garbage, clutching her phone with her perfectly manicured hand. Her throat had been ripped out.

I plucked the phone before the screen went dark. It just said Mom.

"Irene!" Loretta lifted a rigid arm to her nose and dropped it. "Unfortunately, her blood is old, and muscles are still stiff. She died last night."

"Let's get the body back inside the coven. We ought to ask Agata to do an autopsy," I said.

"I would think the vampire who ripped out her throat could tell us why he or she or they did it," Loretta said a little too brightly as she showed the bite marks.

"Can we be sure it's a vampire?" Norma asked.

"Who else would it have been?"

"Loretta, Gavin knows Irene."

"We all know Irene."

"Yes, but I'm wondering if Gavin staked Xiao. Maybe Irene was trying to warn us."

"Darling, I saw her nearly every night until she and

Ryan broke up. She said hateful things, even striking our honorable brother.

"I speak most assuredly; Irene wouldn't have warned us of anything. "

LORETTA GENTLY CARRIED IRENE'S BODY into the clinic and set the corpse on an empty gurney. She straightened her clothing and combed the woman's hair with her fingers.

"What is this?" Agata asked, bleeding into Xiao again.

"We found Irene in a dumpster." Loretta glided to her Firstborn and gently took his hand. "I'm helping Norma solve the crime. How are you feeling?"

While Xiao scribbled his answers to Loretta, I asked Agata to autopsy the body.

"Why? It's obvious she was killed by a vampire," Agata said.

"And put in a dumpster," Loretta added.

"Yes, our vampires would have ensured she got a funeral," Agata said. "I can't imagine many of the old rogues would be throwing garbage in our dumpster. How many young rogues are in Seattle?"

"Several, but they hang out in the hipper neighborhoods," I said.

"Georgetown is going through a revival." Agata removed the needle from her arm and carefully bandaged her wound. I noticed the bruising in the small of her elbow didn't disappear immediately. That wasn't a good sign.

Loretta kissed her son's brow. She and I left the clinic together.

"Why do you think Xiao had Ryan's knife?" The elder vampire asked as we strolled along the commercial hallway.

"Ryan said he lost it."

"Marion saw your face. And I'm looking at you now.

You know he lied or at least told a half-truth. And you've been developing a theory."

"I heard a few whispers one of the thralls was having an affair."

"Fern?"

"Yeah." I paused. "You are quite angry. Do you think you can question calmly?"

"Of course, dear one, I always planned to be the good cop."

"Should we tell Derrik what we're doing?"

"I'm not that good of a cop. Besides knowing him, he'd say it's too dangerous."

I giggled.

"What's funny?"

"Just the idea Derrik would tell another elder vampire that something was too dangerous."

Loretta smiled. "Even in the Victorian Era, he was always a bit of a wet-blanket."

I STOOD BEHIND HER AS LORETTA KNOCKED on Ryan's door. He answered wearing casual clothing-sweats and a tank top.

"Lady Loretta, Norma, how may I help you?"

"We must ask you questions." Loretta stepped closer to him.

He glanced sideways at me, but let us into the gray apartment which seemed even gloomier than it had last night. He opened his fridge and poured glasses of cow's blood.

"I hope all our suspects are so hospitable," Loretta said brightly.

"I'm a suspect?" Ryan's hands shook as he set down the cups of blood and sank onto his couch.

"Of course," Loretta said brightly. She took a sip of blood. "Did you know Irene's fate?"

"She left me, Lady Loretta."

"Yes, but she came back last night," Loretta said.

"She did?"

"Yes, Norma and I found her body. Maman will be autopsying it just like in the movies."

Bloody tears swam in Ryan's eyes. "I didn't know. I haven't spoken to her in weeks."

"Can you show us your phone?" I asked.

"For what purpose?"

"Obviously to prove you didn't call her last night. I'm the good cop." Loretta leaned close to Ryan's face and stared into his eyes with her magnifying glass.

Ryan did his best not to flinch away; he failed. He tossed his phone on the table at me.

I went to the recent call history. "Ryan made no calls to Irene. In fact, in the last three months, he has only called Derrik."

"Why did Xiao have your knife?" Loretta asked.

"I already told Marion, I lost it."

Loretta turned toward me. It was time to be the bad cop.

"Lost it with Fern?" I asked.

He narrowed his eyes. "How dare you accuse me? I thought you were on my side even if you are playing the bad cop."

"I am on your side. I'm not accusing you of anything, but we need to know the truth in order to clear you."

I realized Loretta had dominated his mind. Rapidly blinking, he gulped as he tried not to speak the words she pulled from him. "I can't tell you what's going on between me and Fern, but I won't stop her from telling you."

"Did you stake Xiao?" Loretta asked so coldly I felt it.

"No!"

"Did he lie?" Her icy blues eyes pierced my soul.

"No. Ryan did not stake Xiao, but I've already said

that."

"Did you stake him, bad cop?" Loretta grabbed my wrist. "Are we to have a twist ending?"

"No. I'd never hurt a vampire of the coven."

Loretta looked at Ryan. "Did she lie?"

Loretta just made a play! *Wow. She really had been watching a lot of cop movies.*

"No. She told the truth," Ryan said.

"Good. Let's speak to Fern," Loretta said.

ORETTA KNOCKED ON XIAO'S APARTMENT door. Fern answered wearing sweats. Her eye shadow was smudged, and mascara ran down her cheeks.

"Hi, Fern," I said. "Did you hear the news? Xiao will recover."

"I didn't stake him." She still held the door. "I swear it, Lady Loretta."

Loretta took a step forward and met Fern's gaze. Leaving her front door open, Fern backed into the apartment in a trance. We were bending the HOA rules, but I didn't plan on snitching. If we were caught, Lady Loretta did not care about a fine when her son was in agony as his skin stitched itself slowly back together in a fight for his undeath.

"I'm not saying you did. We wanted to ask how you and Xiao are doing."

Fern gestured for us to sit. Loretta sat on the sofa.

I pointed at the bathroom. I kept the door open so I could hear the conversation as I poked through the hamper. Nothing was torn or missing fabric. The dress which Fern had worn on the Sabbath was hanging undamaged from the retractable clothesline in the shower.

"We had a lover's quarrel. Xiao knew I was leaving him, but I wouldn't have killed him," Fern said.

I went into the suite and poked through Fern's closet

for a torn dress. This was another dead end.

"Why were you planning to leave him?" Loretta asked.

"He didn't love me, but kept making jealous accusations, Lady Loretta."

I returned to the living room and shook my head at Loretta who asked, "Were you having an affair?"

"No, of course not." Fern's wavering voice held an undertone of fury.

Loretta glanced at me.

"She told a falsehood," I confirmed. "Not even an emotional affair?"

"No. I don't need to answer these questions." Her whole body trembled.

Loretta narrowed her eyes. "You do. Or you can leave the coven."

"You can't put me out on the street. I have tenant rights. You need to give me 90 days."

"This modern era will be the death of me," Loretta stood up and turned her back on Fern. "Of course, I could take your blood. I could bend your will to mine and spark your nerve endings. It will hurt, but it doesn't leave physical damage and as you've already told us, Xiao won't mind."

I noticed Fern glanced at the calendar on the wall. It was a picture of a gray kitten playing with red, white and blue streamers. Was that a clue? Probably not. The Sabbaths were circled. There was also a doctor's appointment- for a doctor outside the coven. Maybe that was a clue.

"Please sit down, Loretta. We need to remain calm." I mouthed, "Good cop."

With her old world manners, Loretta prettily retook her place on the couch.

"Why did you go to the doctor?" I asked. "Are you sick?"

"Just a physical."

"Are you pregnant?" Loretta asked. She looked excited

by the possibility. Even though it meant Fern had an affair with a human.

"No."

Loretta screamed, "Did you do it? Did you try to kill my son because he knew you are pregnant?"

"Loretta, this is not being the good cop at all. You're ... badgering the witness." I knew that wasn't exactly what Loretta was doing, but it sounded good.

Loretta sat and calmly asked: "What's your relationship to Ryan?"

Fern tilted her head. She opened her mouth, and no sound came out.

"That's why Xiao had Ryan's knife, isn't it?" Loretta asked. "While Xiao was at work, you and Ryan had a little tete-a-tete? You were giving Ryan your blood?" She continued.

Silence. We waited.

"Xiao found Ryan's knife in my room." Fern took a deep breath and wiped her stained face with the back of her hand. "But it wasn't like that. I love him, and he loves me. I'm entering the program. I went to the doctor to get a clean bill of health."

Loretta's frown turned into a smile. "Is that all? Why did you hide it?" Loretta cupped the young woman's face and kissed each cheek.

Fern did not expect to be kissed and her lies hung on her shoulders, pushing her deeper into the chair.

"I was so young when I became a thrall. I came to the coven a runaway hoping to find a life. I used to think Xiao was all moody and mysterious, but that's no way to live. He hides his feelings and keeps them all bottled up."

"My son..." Loretta's lips trembled. She didn't like what Fern was saying, but she didn't stop her from saying it.

"Lady Loretta, I like Xiao. He is kind to me and I've tried to be kind to him, but our existence was not quite right. Neither of us is truly happy, but Xiao's so traditional he would never ask me to leave though he doesn't care for me.

"I've been hiding in the coven as a thrall for years, but I'm in agony. I didn't see any way out. I didn't know how to explain the gap in my employment or even find a job. I wanted to ask Jakub for help, but I didn't want everyone to know my disillusionment.

"Especially after how Ryan and Irene broke up. It was so bitter."

"Then one night, I ran into him in the parlor. We talked for hours. He was a perfect gentleman. I realized I don't want to be a thrall; I want to be a vampire. But I have no money of my own. No condo. Xiao pays for everything."

Loretta took her hand. "Was Ryan going to turn you?"

"We hadn't decided. We thought we might ask one of the elders. I figured you and Charles wouldn't because of my history with Xiao, but maybe Derrik or Pascaline would."

"You are an intelligent and beautiful woman, we would be honored to have you as a daughter. There was no reason to hide from us. Any of us."

Fern's mouth opened up in a surprised "O." She sniffed. "Lady Loretta, I wasn't hiding from the vampires. Not even Xiao. He'll understand. I was hiding from the thralls."

"The thralls?" she asked.

"The enthralled treat other enthralled who join the program like we are gold diggers. Or power-hungry monsters. So Ryan and I weren't going to say anything until I found a job and could join as an initiate and get my own apartment. If Ryan and I were meant to be together, we would be together as vampires."

Since I knew she could not lie and had not, I said, "That's pretty romantic and I would be honored to call you my coven sister."

"Indeed, as would I." Loretta kissed Fern's cheeks again.

Chapter 15

4 AM

LORETTA AND I WALKED ARM IN ARM. OUR next stop was to speak to Ethan. However, the small efficiency apartment was still empty. The dishes had been washed and put away. The bed had been made. We went deeper into the Sanctum, which was also still empty except Pascaline in her coffin.

I pressed my fingers to my eyebrow as I sensed an erratic mental image. "Someone is nearby. I can't tell if it's Pascaline or someone else."

"I sense nothing."

"It's gone now anyway."

Loretta looked upon the glass coffin. "How much I miss you, dear sister."

"I miss you too." I looked down.

Pascaline's black nightgown set off her pale white arms which were stretched out beside her.

"Her hands are in a different position than when I last was down here. Do you think it's possible that she has awoken?"

Loretta side-hugged me. "No, she has not. When a vampire awakens from torpor, they have a bloodlust that must be satiated."

"Then why move her hands?"

"Perhaps, Ethan was just cleaning? He is rather

fastidious," Loretta said.

I could not argue with that. We moved up the stairs toward Pascaline's apartment. Ethan wasn't there either.

We turned to check the garage, but on the staircase, Jakub carried Agata in his arms.

Loretta and I spoke together: "Maman/Bunică, what's wrong?"

Jakub said, "She's exhausted. She's been giving too much blood trying to heal Xiao. She collapsed in the clinic. Loretta, I left Michella with Xiao. You and Charles need to keep him safe."

Loretta hurried to the clinic; I followed Jakub to Agata's apartment. Bernie and Kuma were playing checkers. They both stood as the vampires entered.

"What happened?" Kuma asked.

"Ready her coffin," Jakub ordered.

Bernie ran into her coffinroom.

Her heavy, cherry wood coffin smelled of the lemon pomades which she kept with her jars of old Earth. Its glossy finish and brass handles glimmered in the dim light, reflecting across the room casting golden patterns on the wall. The light hypnotized me for a moment and I felt out of my body. *This cannot be happening! If Agata falls ill, who knows what will happen to the coven!*

I pushed my fear back down into my stomach. Even if my shell looked young, I was the eighth oldest vampire in the coven. I needed to remain composed and reassure the younger vampires.

Jakub laid Agata on the tufted rose-colored velvet. Kuma adjusted her feet and pulled off her shoes. He set a thin satin quilt over her.

"How much blood did you give, Lady Agata?" Bernie asked.

"Too much. She always gives too much to the children," Jakub said.

Kuma took her bleeding knife from her dressing table and opened his wrist.

"You gave Norma blood less than two nights ago," Jakub snarled at him.

"Lady Agata's undeath is my life." Kuma pressed his wrist to her mouth. "I would die for her."

Out of instinct, Agata sucked his wrist. Her eyes, full of dark and alien strength, opened. Kuma moaned. Her irises ringed with red before intelligence returned. She pushed Kuma's wrist away.

"Enough. I can't bleed you more, Kuma." Her voice was a feeble whisper. "I won't weaken you. I...blood...in."

Then she closed her eyes again.

Kuma appeared disappointed, but he went to the dressing table and carefully bandaged his wrist.

"Don't look so distraught, my friend. She's wise not to weaken you," Jakub said. "You and Bernie are her last line of defense if something should happen to me."

"Ryan's been drinking the stored blood," Kuma snapped. "And who knows how much Xiao's been drinking with his injury."

"True, but there's still plenty of animal blood in the pantry," Jakub said in a calm, slow manner of one who had existed over five hundred years. "I don't like how this week has been, so you and Bernie must protect Agata's body. Day and night. I want one of you with her.

"And you, Norma, must help Marion solve this crime. Put aside your distrust of your sister."

I FOLLOWED KUMA DOWN TO THE PANTRY, passively listening to his emotions and thoughts. His face remained blank, but he raged inside. He wondered if Fern had staked Xiao and hated her for her infidelity. Not because he cared about Xiao, but because Agata cared so much for all her vampire offspring.

"Are you all right?" I asked him.

"No, I'm not all right! I gave you blood instead of my glorious lady."

"Yeah, I never thought this could happen."

"Who did?"

He opened up a refrigerator with so much power that the bags inside jiggled and sloshed. "Jakub's wrong."

Several bags were taken, and there were many empty spaces on the racks. I glanced at the clipboard which showed who accessed the blood. Ryan had taken weekly bags of human blood and daily cow and deer blood, but it was all accounted for.

"Uh oh," I showed Kuma the list.

"Freaking vampires! Sometimes I think you don't respect all we thralls do to keep your undeath comfortable. I bleed into bags for you and don't get anything out of it. I check the shutters every night, set the daylight clocks."

"I'm sorry, Kuma, what can I do to help? Do you think Agata tried to pump blood into Xiao? If she got weak..."

"How dare you speak of Lady Agata in such a way? After all she has done for you, you call her a thief?"

"No, I don't mean stole ... I mean in a hurry grabbed it. Due to all Xiao's needs, maybe it slipped her mind to fill out the form. Maybe she meant to send someone over to do the paperwork for her."

"Lady Agata would never do such a thing. She is a Walking Goddess." He grabbed a bag of deer's blood and the last bag of blood which had his name on it, slammed the door shut, and stormed out.

I reopened the door and studied the missing blood. It was human blood that had gone missing, mostly Ethan's, Kuma's, Bernie's. There was still plenty of cow, deer, and pig blood and there was one bag of Fern's left and one bag of Summer's. Ryan would grow hungry if he didn't get some money. Maybe I should offer him a job again. Or Derrik would feed him.

I APPROACHED THE SECURITY DESK. MARION immediately crossed her arms and legs and slid the chair in front of the computer. Her mouth was downturned somewhere between a frown and a sneer. "I'm busy. What do you want?"

"My honored sister, in the pantry — "

"Taking more than your share?" Marion snapped.

"No. I wasn't taking anything. Agata fainted. Kuma wanted to nourish her. We noticed several pints have gone missing."

"Are you calling your siblings thieves?"

"No, honored sister, I'm only informing you of something I witnessed. Jakub said to put aside my distrust and work with you."

The sneer went upward into a smirk, but Marion's lips remained closed. I sensed I was still approaching Marion all wrong. I didn't know how to make it right. I didn't have any idea how to reach someone with such a closed mind.

Marion clenched her elbow so tightly, her pale fingertips went gray. "Jakub is not of my bloodline. He cannot tell me what to do. You and I are not going to work together. Besides, I already know who staked Xiao."

"Tell me, honored sister?"

The hair on my neck stiffened as Marion's icy hand patted mine.

"You know, my coven's shame, I wish you had done it. It's too bad you are unfortunately as honorable as any vampire — even if your maker wasn't. Leave me to my work."

Chapter 16

4:37 AM

AFTER SEEING DERRIK WAS NOT AT HIS office, I raced up the stairs to his apartment. His red eyes peered up from his bible at my arrival. "What happened now?"

"Marion says she knows who did it," I panted.

"Did she say who?"

"No. But she knows it wasn't me."

"Thank God for that."

Yet I sensed anger all around me and I sensed it was growing. I focused to ensure it did not overwhelm me.

Derrik's old landline phone rang; he answered it. Whatever tinge of color left in Derrik's ivory flesh disappeared, and his arms slipped around his own body. Blood glistened on his brow.

Outside the apartment, I felt soft vampiric footsteps and angry voices in the hallways.

Bloody tears leaked from his eyes and trailed down his cheeks as he set down the phone in its cradle. "Loretta called. The coven decided Ryan was guilty."

"We have to get him out of here," I said.

"It's too late."

I heard the noise growing in the hallway. I peeked out the front door.

Marion led the offspring of Charles and Loretta who

pulled Ryan and Fern out of Ryan's apartment. Ryan wasn't wearing a shirt; Fern was wearing a flimsy garment that might be a slip, nightgown or summer dress.

"What are you doing?" I called at the backs of the vampires.

Marion's voice rang out over the others: "Ryan Robert Jones, you have been found consorting with an enthralled human contracted to another vampire. You are..."

"Stop this. You didn't have a vote. My vote wasn't counted," I cried.

"A vote is a formality. We have the votes," someone said.

"Ryan couldn't have done it," I shouted. "Michella, don't do this. Tabitha! Vera!" I tried to call to those who showed me any friendliness in the past few days though they weren't turning toward me. "Please, we need to have a vote!"

"His knife was found on Xiao," Marion shouted. "Irene is dead; Xiao has been staked. Fern was caught in his apartment. Neither of them was dressed."

I tried to push my way to my coven brother. A man's hands shoved me backward, hard enough I lost my footing. I cried out then. Before I hit the floor someone else grabbed me and put me upright. It was Jeffry, one of Charles's sons.

"My honored sister, don't make a scene." Then he pushed me toward Derrik.

I hated being smaller than other vampires. I was about three times stronger than the average fourteen-year-old girl, but Charles's sons had all started as powerful men, soldiers, who grew more powerful with every passing decade.

Fern cried as three vampires lifted her off her feet.

"Let her go," Ryan bawled, bloody tears streaming down his face.

I turned around: "Derrik, Loretta, please do something!"

At the end of the hall, not moving toward Ryan, Loretta

and Charles comforted Derrik who wept into his hands. I wished we had found clues to exonerate Derrik's Secondborn. Instead we made him seem more guilty.

I opened my mind. Loretta was impatient for action, but she didn't agree with arresting someone without a vote. She was too calm and collected to show any anger at the proceeding. Still, she followed the will of the coven. They had the votes.

Charles was angry. He also didn't agree with arresting someone without a vote, but someone made his wife cry. Someone pained her by harming her-no, *their*- son.

Derrik was beside himself with grief. This was Bill all over again. Marion and her riot were correct: they had the votes.

I appealed to logic. "That only means Xiao had the knife, not that Ryan did anything wrong."

Ryan's soul pleaded beyond me to Derrik. "Get Jakub!" He screamed. I tried to wedge my way closer.

This time Michella and Vera pushed me back. "Get out of here, Norma. Take care of Derrik."

"Did you stake Xiao?" Someone yelled.

"Tell us the truth, or we will refill the pantry with Fern's blood," Another voice shouted.

Ryan's posture sagged. "Fern and I had an affair. I love her; Xiao doesn't. But I didn't stake Xiao! I wouldn't stake my coven brother and friend."

"You can't go around accusing people," I cried. "We have no real proof Ryan staked Xiao. We only know Ryan and Fern had an affair. It's not even logical. The window was smashed open. That means it must *not* have been a vampire."

"So you think Fern did it on her own?"

"No!"

"It could have been both of them together. Fern has no respect for Xiao if she's flaunting her body to Ryan," Marion hissed.

"It could have been a stranger. I'm saying don't jump to conclusions. It's only been two nights," I said.

"Two nights and a staked vampire and a dead thrall!"

"Both that lead to Ryan!"

I wasn't sure which vampires were shouting justifications for what they were doing as their noisy thoughts pounded my mind, but even ten paces away, I could hear the slight grinding of Derrik's fangs and the click of his jaw.

I chased after the group and squeezed myself between vampires to get up the stairs. It was so crowded. I was jostled into shoulders of grown men and was pushed back again.

I yanked my phone from my pocket and texted: I need you and my van. EMC.

Carlos: So much for PTO. Be there in thirty.

Above me on the stairs, it looked like Ryan might have fainted or perhaps had lost his footing. Marion and the sons of Charles dragged him up the stairs to the roof. At the door, he tried to grab the handrail. Though he looked stronger than the lithe woman, Marion yanked him off his feet and pushed him on to the roof. Four other vampires jumped on him and dragged him to the patio furniture.

The daughters of Loretta brought along Fern.

"This could destroy the coven. Don't do this!" I cried as I emerged onto the roof behind the others. Four vampires tied Ryan onto a chaise lounge with a thick, coarse rope, knotted several times. *Thank God for small miracles.*

"Norma, stop being melodramatic," Tabitha snapped.

Marion put her hands on her hips. "Ryan, confess, and maybe we will be merciful." Her lips spread into a smile.

I itched to punch that smile off her face, but violence wouldn't help Ryan. I stood in front of him.

"Please, don't do this. Don't hurt my coven brother."

"What do you care? You don't even reside here," Marion said.

"Think of Derrik!" I replied. It was all I could think to

say.

"This won't destroy the coven, Norma," Derrik said softly. "If my sons are dead, I will leave. You can stay or go as you wish. You ought to stay."

"I wouldn't side with the coven. This is wrong."

"No more wrong than the shame you bring by your very presence," Marion said. "If I had my choice, we'd tie you up to the rope as well and end the shame of the line of Derrik."

That shifted the mobs sentiment somewhat, but not enough. I refused to give ground, though my knees felt watery as I stared down the wall of merciless vampires. My icy bones shivered in my flesh. Every nerve ending sparked as their anger washed over me. If I were to die, I would die as Bill died. I would die facing my enemies bravely.

"Enough," Loretta said. "Norma's Cleaning Service is the most profitable subdivision of the Paper Flower Consortium. If you force her out, all of our association dues will have to be raised. Derrik also brings money into the coven with his legal practice — consider what you do."

"I'm bringing a murderer to justice," Marion said.

The crowd of vampires cheered.

"I'm not a murderer. I had an affair with another vampire's thrall. I confessed that," Ryan said. "Please let me go."

"We'll see what you say as dawn's light crests the horizon," Marion said.

"Oh, God. Let me go," Ryan cried.

"Yes, you are in God's hand's now," Loretta said. I felt the pull of my will in her words.

"If God wants you to survive, maybe he'll send an angel," Marion said.

The women tied Fern to a chaise lounge and positioned it so to watch Ryan as he burned. Unless wind pushed the flames onto her chaise, she would be extremely dehydrated and sunburned by the end of the day and suffer watching

Ryan burn, but she would live.

Once Fern was secured, Vera and Tabitha grabbed me by the arms. "Norma, come along, don't make a scene. There are too many who would like to see you stay up here," Vera said.

"But..."

"Hush." Tabitha said.

"For once in your undeath, do as your coven commands." Vera hugged me into her chest and forced me to walk. When I didn't, I was dragged. For dignity's sake, I walked. "You obviously love our coven brother very much, but you can't help him now."

"Only an angel can help him," Michella repeated Marion's words.

ONCE THE DOOR TO THE ROOF WAS SLAMMED shut and chained from the inside. Derrik's eyes fell to his shoes. In silence, he shuffled down the stairs. As if in a nightmare, he wandered into his apartment and lay on the couch. He found a box of matches and held them.

I knelt in front of him. "I'll find a way to save Ryan."

"There's no way to save Ryan. This is Bill all over again." Still clutching his matches, he rolled over to face the back of the couch. "The best we can do is protect ourselves. And leave when we are able, but not too quickly or we will be dishonored."

"What if I awoke Agata?"

"She cannot help us."

He looked emotionally and physically exhausted. I covered him with a blanket. There was little doubt that Loretta had dominated him to protect her and Charles's offspring.

Since he couldn't help, I went down to the security office and knocked on the door. I had to talk sense into someone.

"What do you want?" Marion looked pleased with herself.

Still, I had to try. "Marion, why are you interested in Ryan? I know he was Irene's lover but what does he gain by killing her?"

"You claim you heard men's voices arguing right before you found Xiao. Keith and I believe your theory the violence is nearly unknown to the coven. Irene is dead, and the fact that Xiao was staked is abnormal. It must be the same guy," Marion said. "The only person who might have done it is Ryan ... or Derrik. After all, he is the one who brought shame to the coven, by changing William, now Ryan. Are you saying I should look closer at him instead?"

"But I know it's not Ryan," I said. "The broken window?"

"Are you willing to take his place?"

"I don't see why you are in a rush to find a solution?"

Marion barred her fangs. "Are you stupid? You who claim to solve problems and clean up messes. Do you know what I had to clean up?

"Seven thralls sent in their resignations once Agata collapsed. Michella and Vera were talking about going over to Bellevue. They have initiates to be changed next year. My own mother didn't trust me to do my job."

I felt the truth in Marion's words. "You're wrong. Loretta wanted us to work together. She chided me for not working with you," I said.

"Work with the Paper Flower Consortium's shame? My job is to protect the coven. Don't you get that?"

Marion's expression changed from one of anger immediately into what I recognized as her professional security face. Her mind grew harder to read unless I opened my mind wider and chance hearing everyone.

I would not receive any further information. Besides

Marion was so true to the coven though she loathed me, she wouldn't harm the coven by throwing me on the roof. She had circumstantial evidence of Ryan's misdoings. It was enough.

I finally understood. While I had been looking for the truth, Marion had been trying to protect the coven as a whole. If I had only listened to Jakub or Loretta.

Loretta. She dominated Derrik in order to keep things calm—but she hadn't been pleased about it. What if she was still my ally?

I raced to the parlor. Loretta's long ivory fingers played the harp. The gentle music rested upon my brow like cool water. Jakub, Charles and her offspring, the several initiates, (minus Xiao and Marion) sat around the room listening to her. *Was she dominating them in the softest way possible?*

There is a tinkling of laughter in the far corner of the room as someone bit into the neck of their enthralled human. In the parlor, the coven was returning to normalcy, even as a vampire and a thrall were tied to the roof.

"Loretta," I asked.

"How dare you address my lady mother in such a fashion?" Michella hissed.

Loretta raised her hand. "I gave my permission and never rescinded it, though I wouldn't think I would have to spell out such things to Derrik's bloodline."

"Lady Loretta, I heard an argument which means this couldn't have been an accident. Very few vampires could stake Xiao in the chest. When Charles and I were in the infirmary, I felt bloodlust. It was hard to be focused. There was blood everywhere. If it was a vampire... they would have still been there on the stairs."

The gilded clock in the parlor rang throughout the hallways to warn one hour to sunrise. It was set each day by the most trustworthy of thralls. I hadn't heard the sunrise clock the morning Xiao was staked, but maybe I had come to ignore it as I did when I was a girl. Since Derrik was a bit of a helicopter parent, I always knew the time.

"So what are you saying?"

"I am begging you: Marion said maybe an angel would save him. Let me be Ryan's angel. If he did commit the crime, I will bring him back here to face the coven's judgment, but if he didn't, let us show him mercy. We must not rush, but ensure we look at all the options."

"I grant it. None of my children will stop you." There was grumbling and two threats on my undeath, one on my person. "However, if God wants you to save him, He will let you through the lock. None will help you either."

Though there were angry grumbles, not a single vampire or thrall rose from their seats. Loretta domination spell was too complete.

Loretta couldn't have stopped the mob on the roof, but she had planted a suggestion. She gave someone an opening — knowing one vampire would storm the gates.

Chapter 17

5:10 AM

I CHECKED MY PHONE TO DOUBLE CHECK sunrise was 5:28. Damn. There was simply no time.

I raced to the storage closet and searched through the maintenance staff's tools, hoping for a bolt cutter. I found a hacksaw.

I took the steps two at a time, stumbling and scratching my leg. I kept running. If I was lucky, Loretta had calmed the entire coven. If I wasn't, the spell would break, and someone would trap me onto the roof too.

Being a lawyer wouldn't hurt Loretta's children.

I called Derrik. When he answered the phone I shouted: "I'm being an angel, but I might need a lawyer. Carlos is on his way!"

I hung up before he got past the first "Damn..." I knew he would come.

Out of breath, I made a few links taunt and sawed back and forth. Once I made a cut halfway, I pulled with as much strength as I had. The chain didn't break. I kept sawing, slivers of metal fell to my feet. I tried again. This time it snapped.

"What are you doing up here?" Fern cried.

Ryan lifted his head, but his eyes were full of defeat. Darkness discolored the crotch of his pants. The bloody sweat stained his shirt. "I swear I didn't try to kill Xiao."

"I know," I said.

Hope crept into his eyes. "You're here to free us!"

I began to cut through the rope with the hacksaw. Strands gave way one by one.

"You're not supposed to be here?"

"They won't help or hinder us."

"It's almost dawn," Fern cried.

"Yeah. I'm aware."

I kept sawing. More strands frayed.

The vague suggestion of dawn lightened the horizon. I tried to cut quicker. Ryan tugged at the ropes. They snapped free. Now able to sit, he ripped at his bonds. I quickly finished untying him, and we both freed Fern.

The first sunbeams pierced the sky. Ryan screamed and covered his eyes. *Good grief.*

I grabbed his wrist with both of my hands. "Get up. You have to move! Fern, help me!"

At first, Fern and I dragged him toward the door. Ryan started to run, and with his longer strides, he dragged us. He wrenched open the roof door and shoved me and Fern inside. He pulled the door shut behind him.

"Thank you." He smothered my brow and cheeks with kisses as he gave me a bear hug. Fern too was hugging me.

I was both embarrassed and grateful at the reaction. Not even Derrik and Pascaline showered me with this much affection.

"You saved me. Even what I said to you...about you... earlier. You saved me," Fern said.

"Yeah, well, you were just upset about Xiao and not saving you would make Sunday Morning Family Dinners even more awkward."

"You saved him!" Marion's fangs expanded and dripped with saliva. "Them."

I looked down the steps at the wall of vampires who looked up at us.

I whispered to Ryan and Fern. "I wouldn't thank me

yet. Come on. We've got to get to our feet." To Marion, I said, "Wasn't it you who said if God wanted Ryan to survive, he'd send an angel to the roof?"

"Blasphemer." Marion took a step closer.

"Oh, shut it." I thought about Bill again. I needed to push him away.

Carlos and Derrik pushed through the crowd. "Norma, don't tell your coven sister to shut it. It is unseemly."

"Unseemly? Tying an innocent man to the roof is unseemly!"

STOP. Derrik shouted at me with his mind. He was telling me to not escalate the situation. He was right. I must calm down and make them listen. I knew one way, but it was a gamble.

"Besides, I know who the murderer is," I said.

A gasp spread through the assembled crowd.

"But I don't know how I will prove it and make you all believe me."

Ryan squeezed me tighter.

Looking down at the vampires on the stairwell, I stated, "Ryan is innocent of staking Xiao. His only crime is having an affair which he and Fern admitted to and being behind in his HOA dues."

"I've had enough of this," Marion snarled. "Back them up. They'll hit the emergency bar and fall into the sun."

"What Ryan did is wrong, but it is not a death sentence. Declaration 5 subset C clearly states it is a $300 fine for taking another vampire's thrall," Derrik said.

One of Charles's sons shouted a profanity.

Behind us, the door grew ever so slightly warmer. The sun was so close. Our backs were to the door, and Marion was right, if we hit the bar the door would open.

Carlos roared. The sound which came from down his throat was chilling even to me. If I perished, he'd rip down the coven vampire by vampire.

The vampires backed to the walls and opened a path for the shade. Carlos gestured to Derrik again.

"Thank you, as I was saying Declaration 5 subset C clearly states it is a $300 fine for taking another vampire's thrall," Derrik said, climbing the steps to us.

I knew Derrik wouldn't let his offspring down. No matter what. He still loved Bill. He still loved Ryan and me. He clutched Ryan's arm and pulled me close to him. "And as for Norma, there is no declaration at all for saving another vampire who has not faced official coven justice."

"He can't pay the fine." Someone grumbled behind Marion. "And he's over a year behind in his HOA dues."

"He can't pay the fine," Marion yelled. "And we can vote him out."

From the bottom of the stairs, Jakub spoke in his quiet way. "According to our condo bylaws: you can vote him out of the coven, and the debt will follow him until it is repaid, but he cannot be thrown into the sun for these minor offenses.

"Agata commands this door is to remain shut until Norma solves the crime and we *all* are satisfied. If coven justice is warranted, there will be an official vote."

"Then throw him out of the coven," someone shouted. "Let's see if he can find shelter in the city."

"I can pay the fine," I said. "And my coven brother can pay me back."

"You can't do that!" Marion screamed.

"I often make payment plans with my clients."

"He is your coven brother, not a client," Marion said.

"Oh, for heaven's sake, Norma works for coven vampires all the time," Jakub said.

Chapter 18

8 AM

I PACED IN DERRIK'S LIVING ROOM WHICH was now full of people. Derrik, Hugo, Carlos, Ryan, and Fern. I should have solved the mystery already. As it was, my lies only bought a little time.

"Why can't I see it? All the clues seem like dead-ends. The lace was a piece of handkerchief. A commonly used one. Agata, Pascaline, Loretta and all her daughters have one. Apparently, I even have one."

"Wait, my lamb. You sold a dog to the whole of the coven?" Derrik asked. "Do you have any idea what might happen?"

"They wanted to push open the door. I had to buy some time. Ryan's knife was a dead-end. And almost got Ryan killed. As it is we've got to get him out of here."

Are you worried they will throw him back into the sun?" Derrik asked. "Jakub said Ryan is safe."

I couldn't believe a lawyer could be so naïve. "As long as we don't know who staked Xiao, the coven is in peril, and that makes the vampires feel unsafe. It makes us dangerous. Marion was right about that." I pulled out my phone. "I have an idea of where Ryan can go, but old-timey morals might come into play, so Fern should stay here."

"Where?"

"In my room? We can share it."

"You'll sleep in your coffin?" Hugo asked.

"Well, I'm not closing the lid."

"Still an improvement."

"No, I mean where are you going to take my son?"

I didn't answer immediately; instead, I opened my contacts. I bit my lip as I waited for the phone to ring. Betty picked it up on the third ring.

Carlos wrote on a piece of paper.

Laurence's old landlady. She's too old to give a hoot that Laurence was a vampire. We've used her house as a safe house once for a witch who was abused by her spouse.

"Hello?" The raspy human voice whispered into the phone.

"Hi, Betty. It's me, Norma. I hope this isn't too early to call."

"Oh, Norma, so wonderful to hear from you. How is Carlos?" Her voice sounded brighter but still weak.

"He's fine. Still on that paleo thing. I was wondering if you had a tenant?"

"No," Betty said.

"Do you want or need one?" I asked.

"I can't sign any long-term leases. My health."

"Is this a good time for guests?"

"Neither good or bad," Betty said.

"I've a coven member who needs a place to stay. He was created by the same guy who made my maker."

"So that makes him your uncle?" Betty asked.

"Yeah. Kind of like my uncle, but I'm older." I shrugged at Ryan and Derrik. "I can pay you a month's rent for a few days of your time."

Betty sighed. "He's in trouble?"

"Yes."

"What kind of trouble?"

In a gossipy tone that sounded more upbeat then I felt, I said, "You won't believe this, but one of the vampires was staked, and some of the other vampires think it was my sort-of uncle because he and the vampire's wife were playing a little backseat bingo. It's a soap opera over here."

Before Derrik or Ryan could interrupt with the correct vampire vocabulary or freak out that I was talking openly about vampires with a human, I waved them quiet.

"You'll like him. He's a marine biologist. I need a few more days to solve the crime. Figure out who actually did the staking."

"What if I need to go to the doctor ... And what will he eat?" Betty asked.

"I'll bring him a three-day cow's blood supply and a couple steaks. He will pay for any Ubers and knows how to drive so he can take you anywhere you want to go, if it's after sundown, he'll most likely be sleeping all day. He's generous and kindhearted. Never has a bad word to say about anyone."

"Even the man who was staked?" Betty asked.

"Never said a bad word about him either, only fell in love with his wife."

"What happened to the wife?"

"She's under my grandpa's protection right now. She's going to stay in his guest room until this whole thing blows over."

"Well, I'll want to hear the whole soap opera, so he better be a good storyteller."

I gave Derrik and Ryan a thumbs up sign. "Great, thanks! We can be there in an hour."

USING MY GURNEY, DERRIK AND RYAN moved his coffin into the van. Carlos carried his two suitcases. One filled with food raided from Derrik's fridge, the other with clothes and toiletries.

"You are up late?" Jakub wrung his pale hands that were tipped with blood where he chewed his nails--or Agata had.

"We've got to get Ryan out of here, Sir Jakub," I said.

"Some might think it's an admission of guilt, self-proclaimed guardian angel."

"Do you?"

"My dearest children, I've seen nothing but misbehavior between two vampires and a thrall. And the angel who lied through her teeth, because her knightly guardian couldn't break through a domination spell," Jakub said. "Do I have it straight?"

"Yes, Sir Jakub, you do," I said.

"Do you have someplace in mind?" he asked.

"Yes, but I ought not to speak it aloud."

"Yes, dear, you ought not. Be safe, my poor little Ryan." Jakub got on his toes to kiss his brow. "Agata and I love all our offspring."

I climbed into the back seat with Ryan. I was amazed that just by getting in the van, I felt more relaxed than I had in days. I grabbed a tube of sunscreen and smothered myself.

Handing Ryan the tube, I said, "This might be a bad time, but do you mind if I blindfold you. I kind of want to keep the safe house secret."

"What?" Ryan asked.

"Just kidding," I lied.

Chapter 19

9 AM

"**L**OOK AT THIS FINE-LOOKING YOUNG man," Betty said as we scurried inside the door.

Betty's once beautiful brown skin looked sallower than last time I had seen her. Her frizzy gray hair had thinned too. A dark pit in my stomach began to grow: It was as if this once robust woman was disappearing before my eyes.

"It'll be nice to have movement in the house again, even for just a few days. I've had problems finding quality tenants after Laurence moved out. I'm too sick to know when it will end. Now my niece stops by every two days, but she shouldn't be a problem."

"Is she okay with vampires?" Ryan asked.

"As long as we don't tell her. She'd think I'd gone senile and needed assisted living."

I pressed $1,700 into Betty's trembling hand.

"Baby girl, this is too much."

I put her hands up. "With no tenants and the US health care system, I figured things were a bit tight. I said a month's rent. If it makes you feel better, just know I'm not sure how long it's going to take.

"I planned on going back once we got Ryan all set, but if you want me to stay, I will."

"Come back after you solve the crime," Betty said. "I'll

have dinner with your uncle. This boy has a long story to tell me once he gets moved in."

"I will, I promise."

Carlos carried Ryan's stuff into the basement which had its own entrance as Betty informed him of her house rules. The windows still had the thick curtains Laurence left behind. That was good. Ryan would be pretty safe there.

"Why does everyone love Laurence?" Ryan asked as he unpacked his bag and hung his clothing in the closet.

"Betty loves him because he used to keep an eye on her."

"How so?"

"She has trouble breathing after laying down. She can't sleep, putters around at night. Laurence made her cups of tea, talked to her. I hoped you might do that too."

"Great. I never thought I'd be caring for an elderly woman."

"Not even your thrall?" I asked. *No wonder Irene left.*

"Your unspoken thoughts show your ignorance of adult relationships," he snapped.

I wanted to say: *Derrik always takes care of his thralls and their relations in old age.* Still, we were both too emotional to have a logical discussion, so I dropped it with an insincere "Sorry."

Careful not to scratch the floor, we pushed the bed over and put the coffin next to the wall. It made the room a little tight, but Ryan said it was comfortable enough.

"I promise I'll be back to pick you up as soon as I solve this crime. It'll be like a vacation. Maybe it'll even clear your head and help you think about what you want to do next." I felt him tense before his hand formed into a fist.

"Why are you white-knighting me?" Ryan said slowly.

"Dude, I'm not."

"Yes, you are."

Not wanting to shout or alert Betty to anything wrong,

I opened my mind. Ryan accepted my thoughts.

I am not doing this for you, I'm doing this for Derrik. I can never repay everything he did for me. The entire coven wanted me dead, and he took me in. I couldn't bear it if something happened so Derrik didn't want to exist anymore. If you met your Final Death so might he.

Without warning a little voice, underneath my main thoughts, cried: *And I want to prove I'm not the undead shame of the Paper Flower Consortium!*

Ryan took my hand. And as overwrought and overtired I was, I found I couldn't just shut my emotions down again. My mind was out of control and completely spilling into Ryan.

My heart aches knowing Betty's going to die and there's nothing I can do for her. I keep reading stories about how humans must choose between medicines and food. Why doesn't America have Universal Health Care? Derrik went through something like this back when he was human. I wish I remembered my childhood better. There were so many lean years. I feel like the house knows Betty's dying. It smells different here or something.

How can you not feel it?

And the little voice cried: *I hate how other vampires and thralls look at me. I was called an abomination just yesterday. And you think* my *brain is under-developed.*

And under that voice, another voice whispered: *And I'm afraid you're right.*

Derrik and I have never been able to accept someone's emotional state, but Ryan sat down on the bed and pulled me to sit beside him. He put his arm around me. "Okay, it's okay. I get it. That shame of the Paper Flower Consortium crap sucks. No wonder you don't hang out with vampires. Thanks for helping Fern and me. But you should really talk to Derrik about Bill. He isn't ashamed of the relationship at all. And certainly not of you."

"We can't talk about Bill, without one of us crying. Still too much grief about it on both sides. We might never be able to talk about it."

Carlos used his phone's speaker to ask: **Are you okay?**

Ryan answered, "Norma just needs a good day's sleep. And so do I. Our gifts are slipping."

Ryan gave me one more squeeze and then stood up to shake Carlos's hand and that bro-hug thing men do. "Thanks, Carlos, for all you've done for our family."

C ARLOS DROVE ME TO MY CONDO ON Capitol Hill. The cheerful yellow walls rose up to a sky-blue tray ceilings surrounded by crown molding which I had installed and painted myself lightened my spirit. Maybe it wasn't a real sky with a real sun, but it was mine. I ensured nothing was rotting in the fridge and took out the garbage. My apartment cleaned, I took a hot shower, dressed in my pajamas, and lay down on my soft bed. Carlos lay on my couch and turned on the television. I set the alarm and took a four-hour snooze, getting deeper sleep than I had for days.

In my dreams, Bill loomed over me and called me stupid and lazy. He screamed about how I wasted blood. Instead of striking me, Bill staked me through the heart. He ripped it out and stabbed me again, multiple times.

My alarm woke me one hour before dawn. My skin was covered in bloody sweat. Staring at the ceiling I thought: *Maybe Carlos and I could get out of Seattle. Maybe I could become a rogue vampire. I might not have the physical prowess to frighten other vampires away, but I have made enough connections in the supernatural community. Even if the Paper Flower Consortium keeps the business, it can't keep my abilities to clean up messes. Maybe I could move to Portland, or even farther.*

I always wanted to go to Europe and see the places Pascaline and the other vampires talked about. I spoke French. Maybe I could go to France.

Carlos probably wouldn't want to go to France with me. He wouldn't leave his cats.

Carlos knocked on my door.

I rolled out of bed and let him in.

Carlos: **Bad dreams?**

"Yeah." I packed a few extra things for a longer stay at the coven. Realizing if I wanted to return by sunset, I didn't have time to shower, I drove back in pajamas. The outfit looked like shorts and a t-shirt, but the blood was apparent. I drove carefully, fearing getting pulled over.

Sometimes when I drove, I saw the old city. I expected old dance halls and movie palaces that no longer existed. I would sometimes remember older street names. And in a moment of nostalgia, I might scan a crowd and see the women wearing primarily dresses, the men in suits. But, of course, no one dressed like that anymore -especially not on a hot summer day. Sometimes I miss it. Mostly I did not.

With no traffic this early on the highway, we arrived in thirty minutes. Derrik waited for us in the garage. He was scandalized by my attire. He didn't say anything, but he took off his jacket and covered me with it. "Who saw you?"

"No one, but I had to get back."

"What happened to you?"

"Bill haunted my dreams."

He grimaced and rubbed his chin. "Is Ryan all settled?"

"I think so. I hope he's kind to Betty. She's a very nice lady. You'd like her. She has old manners. I will be sad when she dies. It hurts my heart just thinking about it."

"You have a compassionate temperament. I brought Fern into my home, so I hope you were sure about sharing your room."

"I can handle sleeping in my old coffin for a few days,"

I said more confidently than I felt.

Carlos dug through his overnight bag. He held three jars of kitty litter covered with a little dirt and mossy sidewalk debris.

Carlos: I thought about what Derrik said about someday you might needing my earth, so I made you these. One for your condo, one for here, one for your suitcase. I couldn't find enough dirt around my apartment, so I added kitty litter. It's clay, after all and I've touched it enough.

I laughed. "What a good idea!" More seriously I asked, "Are you okay with that?"

Carlos: If you have earth from here and your mother's garden, then having some from me, it means we're friends, right?

"Yes."

"Anyone or place, Norma feels at home with," Derrik said. "Adults of all species tend to sexualize the need, thralls even more so, but vampires are almost never made from people who are happy with the circumstances they were born into.

"Norma's earth isn't here just for her. She also gave some to me after she grew up and moved out. And her earth from here, is earth from Pascaline and I."

Carlos: It's nice someone will miss me for eternity. Beyond this cool exterior, I worry about rotting away. I lost another chunk of hair this morning and had to wash out my eyes they itched so bad.

I wondered if it was possible to get new donated eyes.

Carlos: I just need more antioxidants in my diet. Focus on the crime.

Wait, first take a shower. You look gross.

"Thanks." I walked toward the bathroom.

I overheard Derrik beg Carlos to ensure my continued safety. Since he wrote down his answer, I could not hear his reply.

163

But I didn't worry about it, because we had been friends since I found him undead under that pool table. And friends help each other through whatever mess existence brings them.

I closed the door and peeled off my clothes. They had more blood on them than I thought. I looked like a horror movie, but there was no hole in my chest.

Chapter 20

7 AM

"WHAT DID YOU DO WITH RYAN? WHAT did you do to that murderer?" Marion screamed as I entered the parlor.

The hair on the back of my neck stood on edge, but I forced myself to stand to my full height of five foot, two inches. I unwaveringly gazed upon the other vampires all clad in black leather and lace and silk. Some might be taller, some might be stronger, they all had better fashion sense, but they were younger than me. Carlos hung back and remained beside Derrik as I had asked of him.

They didn't care about Irene's death at all, it was only Xiao getting staked that mattered to them. Their safety.

"I put Ryan somewhere safe so you don't do something stupid again which might lead to the destruction of the coven. We are here because we trust each other."

"How do we trust you?" Marion screeched. "You have committed a crime of impeding justice. I might throw you into the sun!"

I wanted to remind everyone we were not human and human law didn't apply to us.

I didn't have to. Derrik said: "Vampires have no laws about impeding justice, nor does the Paper Flower Consortium bylaws."

Still, someone might try to impede me. "If you want

to know who staked Xiao, you ought to stay out of my way."

"Who did it?" Vera cried from the crowd.

"I have an idea, but I must prove it. Loretta and I will figure it out how to prove it. I know we will."

Loretta gave me an odd look. A peculiar, fluttery feeling filled my stomach. I was no longer sure I could rely upon Loretta. It wasn't surprising. Older vampires tended to get excited about new things very temporarily or keep an interest for a very long time.

"Was it Marion?" One of Charles's sons said from the back. "Is that why she put the blame on Ryan?"

Inwardly I let the joys of *schadenfreude* wash over me. Outwardly, I frowned at the crowd. "No, of course not." I hoped I was right and sounded like an expert.

"Marion had circumstantial evidence because there is no direct evidence. She tried a gambit which unfortunately did not expose who the killer was. I mean really, my honored siblings, you must have all suspected it was just a gambit. Why else would she have used rope to tie a *vampire* to the roof.

"Solving crimes is so much harder than it is on *CSI* and *Law and Order*. If the other vampires would give us time..."

"Time! How can we give you time when there is a murderer with a stake running around the coven?" a vampire screamed. I couldn't see which one.

"Marion and I need time to go over the clues. I was worried people thinking Ryan was the culprit would take justice into their own hands instead of waiting for a proper vote and it would also help if you all stopped destroying clues." I turned and stormed out with more emotion than I really felt.

Loretta followed. "You will still let me help you?"

"If you want to help, Lady Loretta, I would be glad to accept it," I said.

"I wasn't sure if you wanted me, because of the act of

betrayal which my children brought into the coven. Derrik won't take action against them, but you ... you have always been an enigma."

"I wasn't sure you wanted to help me because your children might not like it. And I never wrote the apology letters Charles told me to."

"Put your energies to solving the crime. Protect the coven," Loretta said.

"I'm seeing the cracks. How do you deal with the cracks?"

"Young vampires are impatient, *ma chérie,* you might want to think fast. I will calm my children as I can, but stay close to Derrik. There is such an intense bond of compassion between you." Loretta clasped my hand and squeezed lovingly. "Thank you for protecting Marion. The coven hasn't had any knights for a long time."

Unlike Ryan, when Loretta mentioned knights, it was a compliment.

Chapter 21

8 PM

ICONTINUED MY PACING, WHILE DERRIK made coffee for Carlos and poured blood for me.

Thank you. You really make a good cup of espresso.

"Kuma says Derrik is the best barista," I said.

He is right.

"I must be missing something. People have motives and some of the clues have logical answers and some don't. But I'm missing something."

From his chair, Derrik said, "You wrote down all those clues. Want to read them to us again?"

I opened my notebook. We slowly went through the clues again until our conversation was interrupted by someone pounded on door.

Since I was closest to the door, I answered it.

"Hugo." Bernie's voice sounded hollow.

Derrik leapt to his feet. "What about Hugo?"

"He's fallen in the garage. Hurt his hip."

I pushed past them and raced down the stairs to the garage. Hugo lay beside his car, shivering. A box of groceries had fallen onto the cement floor. "Can you move? Should I get a gurney?"

He rolled to his side, to push himself into a sitting position. "I saw a ghost."

"Carlos and Derrik are coming. Don't try to get up."

Hugo grabbed onto my shoulders. "Normie, keep Derrik away from the Sanctum, I think the ghost went into the Sanctum. Pascaline is in there! Find Ethan and get her out."

Derrik hurried beside them. "Can you move?" He took one of his hands and helped him to his feet. Hugo made a small groan as he tried to put weight on his injured side.

As if Hugo were as light as a child, Derrik lifted him into his arms. Bernie and I went after the stray cans of groceries. I looked at the box. Hugo had obviously shopped at Costco, but the goods didn't look like a traditional Costco run. There was no meat or cows blood to be seen. I glanced under nearby cars to see if a package had tumbled. None. I looked in the back seat of the car. It was empty.

Meat. Blood. A vampire. Vampires aren't picked up on film. And there are many vampire powers that the coven does not have. It might be anyone.

"Bernie, go into your office. No, up to Agata's and bolt yourself in. It's possibly a vampire. A new one."

"There are no new vampires."

"Let's say this one isn't on the registry. Who knows maybe its simply a rogue who wants to join and doesn't have any manners yet."

He locked up his office and hurried upstairs to Agata's.

I picked up the box of groceries and dashed to Derrik's apartment. I threw open the door and found Derrik kissing Hugo's brow and handing him a cup of soup.

"Hugo, you didn't buy any meat or cow's blood?"

Hugo was shaking terribly as he lifted the cup to his lips. "Of course. What else would you three eat?"

"You said you saw a ghost, are you sure it wasn't a vampire?"

"That is absurd, I know all the vampires who reside here."

"Norma, leave Hugo be," Derrik snapped.

"But meat disappeared! I think..."

"Norma, not now."

Derrik was serious, but so was a new untrained vampire. (Actually so was a new shade or ghost or any supernatural entity.) Carlos met my eyes, waiting to see what I would do.

"If I don't figure this out, all the thralls might die. If Hugo didn't have meat and cow's blood on him, he would be dead."

Derrik sat silently for a few minutes with his fingertips pressed together. His legs stretched out in front of him, crossed at the ankles, uncrossed and crossed again. His gaze directed upward to the ceiling. Then to Hugo.

"Norma, you must take my blood," Hugo said softly.

"I don't want to bleed you. Your hip was injured."

Hugo waved away my protestation. "It's only a bruise. You're only sleeping a few hours at night. And Carlos cannot help you the way I can. Kuma and Bernie will only give blood to Agata until she is well. The other thralls don't know you well enough to trust you. You aren't sleeping, but blood will clear your mind."

There was no reason not to do it except it made me feel weird. Derrik kept that side of himself away from me. And back in 1951, after I was trained enough to take Aldo's blood without supervision, I kept it away from him.

"Do you think Fern might help?" I asked.

"Fern is in enough trouble." Derrik said. "She didn't say so, but someone bit into her."

I wondered if it was the lingering effects of Loretta's domination or if someone else had bitten her.

From the Victorian knife cabinet, Derrik took down an antique ruby encrusted dagger from the sixteenth century. Given to him by Jakub, the knife was the most loved of all Derrik's blades and only used on special occasions. The use of the blade was his way to explain quietly, he would follow whatever plan I came up with if I acted like a vampire. We were going to find the murderer!

"I will drink, but...," I said.

"You'd feel more comfortable if I opened the wound?"

"Yes."

Derrik sliced opened the old scar on Hugo's wrist. He began to drink. He lifted his head after a few seconds, his mouth stained scarlet. His pale skin flushed. His eyes glowed red and the placidness of his normal demeanor was gone.

"Come, drink," Hugo said. "Don't fear, Norma. Clear your mind. You won't see any thoughts I don't want you to see."

That was not true. With his blood flowing through my veins I discovered many things about Hugo. However, nothing unworthy about his character. I never felt more the vampire than when I took blood directly from a victim — even though this was not as exciting as hunting with Bill or going to clubs. Still, I watched Hugo's flesh and listened to his heart, careful not to take too much.

"How gentle and cautious you are, even more so than Derrik. Drink."

I allowed the heartbeat to hypnotize me, focusing my thoughts. The mark on my forehead itched as it healed and disappeared.

I took my fill and went into my room. I lay back in my coffin and closed my eyes. Derrik opened the jar of earth from my mother's house.

No one tried to shut the coffin lid.

I pressed my fingers into the dirt. It was cooler than the room around me. It felt as if I could go on in this single moment forever. Instead, I focused. I thought of each individual clue, each suspect and what I had learned. I heard Hugo's heart beating, the electric impulses inside Carlos, every heartbeat of the coven. Mice in the walls. The skittering steps of spiders. Distant music from Loretta's harp.

Agata fainted.

My eyes fluttered open. Derrik sat beside me and stroked my hair.

"How much did it hurt you when Bill made me?" I asked him.

"What does that matter?"

"Agata fainted --and she is still in her coffin. And Pascaline is alone in the Sanctum." I sat up in the coffin. "You are an elder vampire and you must ensure all who are not part of my plan remain safe."

I knew what I hadn't wanted to see: someone — most likely Gavin — had become a vampire from Pascaline's blood. They had stolen it.

There was no doubt about that, but proving it was the problem. I must speak to Marion as a friend.

Loretta had tried to tell me to solve the crime we needed to be buddy cops, we needed to act like they did in the movies. I might not know who the murderer was, but I knew how to discover who it was. I needed a plan to trap them and I had seen enough movies and television to know how to do it.

Chapter 22

11 PM

WITH A DARK SPOT NO LONGER IN JUST the pit of my stomach, but threatening to overtake my entire digestive system and explode, I went to the security desk. Marion's face was set in the glower which caused creases in her pale brow as she watched her monitors. On the monitor, all ten camera feeds were seen. The other cycled through the images of the entrances.

"Marion, I need your help," I said.

"I'm working."

"I know who staked Xiao and killed Irene. We both know it wasn't Ryan. But you were right: it had to be a vampire. Nothing else makes sense. I even think we both know if it was a vampire checking the monitors the entrance won't work."

"You have no idea what I know." Marion sneered. "You are lucky I wasn't undead when you were reborn. I've read your files. You have too much of Vampire William in you. I would have voted for your Final Death."

"I'm sure you would have, but no matter how much I have of Bill in me, I am not him."

She scoffed. "You call him Bill."

With fresh blood in me, I didn't even have to try to read Marion's mind. I caught snippets of what Marion saw when she looked at me: a weak anti-vampire, a victim. Like so many of the other vampires, Marion transformed so she would never again be victimized.

"I also called him Dad, but for some reason that frightens people even worse. When he made me, he told me he was my father, and he taught me to hunt. I've taken down several victims twice my size. Call me the shame of the coven if you want, there is no shame in me."

"How can you exist without shame?"

"I don't know. Maybe it's because, I didn't ask to be reborn, but I don't regret a single day of my life or undeath. Maybe it's simply because Derrik and Pascaline were great parents." I paused. "No matter what he thinks of my rebirth, Xiao is always kind to me. Maybe that's why I'm trying so hard to solve the crime."

Marion didn't react.

"I have an idea how to prove who staked him, but it won't work without your help."

"It's dangerous to play Nancy Drew," Marion said.

I decided to try humor. "That's okay, my rank isn't even Scooby."

Without moving her unblinking eyes away from the monitors, she snarled with her fangs bared: "Have you talked to Derrik about this?"

"Yes and no. He knows I'm up to something, but Derrik would say it's too unsafe. I know it is dangerous, but you were right for the continued security of the coven, we must solve the murder."

Marion stare penetrated me.

"You told me to go do whatever the hell it is I do: well, I fix things."

"You might be hurt." Marion sighed. "Meddling kid."

Was that a Scooby-Doo reference? I chuckled hopefully.

Marion sat up straighter and turned away from the monitors. She was smiling, her real smile. It was a *Scooby-*

Doo reference! "So, I suppose you have a plan?"

"You will help me?"

"Agata is down. We need action, or the coven might lose several members who aren't behind on their HOA dues. No one, not even Derrik, can stop you from taking action."

"Xiao is sure it wasn't you, so I might as well try it your way."

"Keith arrives when?" I said.

"6 AM," Marion said.

"Wow. He must make bank with summer overtime."

"He does pretty well."

"Good. I don't want to leave the main entrance unattended if our killer tries to escape out the front door. Ask any of the former soldiers to stand with Keith," I said. "I want Carlos in the garage in case they try to escape that way."

July 30, 2019

Chapter 23

6 AM

I HOPED MARION, CARLOS AND KEITH WERE in position as I crept toward the Sanctum. The kitchenette appeared empty as did the bed. I moved down the ramp into the darkness, and the humming of the building above disappeared. The silence of the room was deafening.

My foot touched something substantial, unmoving and hidden under blankets. Something dead. I knelt and discovered Gavin. His hands burnt by a silver chain which he held. His face was twisted into a death mask of agony.

My heart fell.

I had hoped it was Gavin who had stolen the blood for YouTube views. An outsider. Someone who was never trusted.

I smelled the vampire behind me. I felt a tingling in my chest as his heartbeat sped up. Ethan did not fear me; he was excited -- and hungry.

I spun around.

Ethan's smile went stiff as if he were not trying to alarm me. He stood very still. Too still for a living creature. That meant not only did he steal Pascaline's blood, but he had killed himself - or had Gavin kill him.

He wore jeans and a teeshirt but no shoes. And I realized how he was moving unseen. He knew were the cameras were. If he undressed, he would not show up on the cameras. *God, Marion, please be in position.* "Why did you turn yourself?"

He didn't answer, but his mind slipped thoughts to me. Ethan had given up his musical dreams for Pascaline.

Gavin had over a million followers. With another chance for fame, Ethan had drunk Pascaline's blood. And when the video was uploaded, Xiao must have confronted him over the theft. What Ethan didn't know is once he died, the thirst would overwhelm him. He tried to change Gavin for the camera which is what they were doing in Pascaline's apartment. Movies made transforming people into vampires look easy. However, Ethan didn't know how to govern his thirst, not take a dangerous amount of blood, because he didn't go through the three-year program.

And the bloodline feels pain when a transformation is painful.

His leather gloved hand clenched onto my shoulder as his other hand pulled the silver chain out of Gavin's hands.

I tried to retreat. Ethan's hand clung as hard as an iron shackle. I tugged my arm away, but only made an inch before he tightened his grip. He was strong for a newborn vampire: Pascaline was three centuries and had only one offspring, Alice. Her blood would have been potent. Moreover, she was Reborn with celerity.

My hoodie ripped under his vice grip.

"You won't get away with stealing my sister's blood."

"What are you going to do to stop me?"

I stomped on his foot. He snarled as if he did not expect the pain, but he did not let me go. It did as little as it had with Bill so many years ago, but it made him talk.

"Pascaline and I will be together forever. If you behave, I'll let her keep you."

Tilting my neck, I bit his left hand. His vampire blood rose from the wound and into my mouth. I sucked hoping to garner his strength.

With his right, he punched me in the face. I staggered back dazed; he got a hold of me again. He grabbed the chains around my wrist. "I take no pleasure in hurting you." He tugged at the chain. It slipped over my sleeve and touched flesh. For vampires in the bloodline of Agata, the touch of silver feels like touching fire. I cried out as it burned.

"Now, do as I tell you or I'll leave it like that," he snarled.

Crying in pain, I struggled against the chains, the silver branding my skin.

He jerked my hoodie sleeve under the chain, so it wasn't against skin. "You're fortunate you're the beloved of my love."

"Why did you do it? For revenge?"

He still didn't answer. He looped the chain around my wrist again until it was secure. My summer-weight hoodie seemed too thin of a barrier between flesh and silver. I was burnt, but no longer on fire.

"Do you hate Pascaline for separating you from your son?"

Ethan's eyes opened wide. A minuscule amount of his humanity came back in his eyes.

"Gavin was your son, wasn't he? Not your nephew like you told Marion before."

"I don't hate Pascaline. Pascaline would have been my avenging angel if she had been awake, but she sleeps. I tried to wake her. She wouldn't ... couldn't wake. My son ... my son is dead."

"You killed him."

He slapped me across the mouth. "I gave him up for Pascaline. Not that she cared. Even now I feel my heart becoming stone. No one tells you, you lose your heart when you become a vampire. No one tells you about the thirst."

The three-year initiation program would have told

Ethan all those things, but I wasn't willing to get hit again by telling him that. Holding the looped chain, he tugged me deeper into the Sanctum. When I hesitated, he threw me into the dark. I skidded against the concrete floor until I fell against the glass coffin. Another rip in my jeans.

I sensed him trying to decide what to do with me. Ethan hadn't wanted to hurt me. He pulled me to my knees. I felt out of options except to kill him. And I wasn't sure I could. All I needed him to say is he staked Xiao; Marion would appear.

"Why did you stake Xiao?"

He didn't answer.

"I don't understand, why did you stake Xiao?"

"He attacked my son, but as he is a vampire, no one cared."

"I cared."

"And you are an eternal child which no one cares about either," Ethan hissed.

"But Gavin got away."

"He hid in Pascaline's apartment. Xiao somehow found out where he was hiding. He came after us!"

"The cell phone? Because Gavin was uploading to YouTube?" I asked. "Xiao saw it on the network?"

Ethan looked surprised. "I knew I liked you, Norma. It's too bad you are too smart for your own good."

"But why kill Irene?"

"A vampire needs to eat, and I saw her number in Gavin's phone. I helped the coven by eating that abusive deserter. I would have eaten the other one too, but I think the werewolves already did. She didn't answer her phone."

The silver linked chain clanked as I tried to move.

I remembered Bill's barn. *No, I'm not in the barn. I'm in the coven. Ethan is not Bill. He's only irrational like Bill.*

"The other vampires will stop you. Derrik will stop you. Marion will stop you."

Ethan slammed my head into the coffin, cracking the

glass.

Dazed by the pain, I curled into a small ball and reached up to my sticky hair mixed with blood. I no longer saw Ethan at all. "Bill is dead. Bill is dead." I repeated to myself. *Where was Marion?*

Ethan's humanity came back once more. "If Pascaline wakes, she'll be hungry. I'd rather give you to her undead, but if she needs your blood, she will take it. Maybe it's for the best. I killed my son for his blood; she can kill you for yours."

Struggling to master the pain, I slowed my breathing.

Ethan pressed down on my wound, letting blood flow into the cracks of the broken glass. I felt weak. I was losing consciousness. I was so tired.

Marion appeared from the shadows. "Ethan. It's time to pick on someone your own size."

Ethan released me as he spun to face Marion. He attacked with a big overhand punch; Marion was faster on her feet. She dodged. Once he was on his follow through, Marion gripped him by the shoulders and tossed him into the wall.

"Get to your feet, little sister. I told you it was dangerous to play Nancy Drew." Marion ripped the chain from my wrists. She grunted to hold back the agony as the silver blistered her fingertips, but she kept unwrapping until the chain crumpled in pieces on the floor.

Ethan was on his feet again and charged Marion. He knocked her down onto Pascaline's coffin then pummeled her stomach with his fists.

With a surge of inspiration, I covered my palm with my long sleeve. I smacked Ethan with the chain. He screamed as it burned his cheek.

I jumped out of Marion's way as she buried a punch into Ethan's nose. Once he was on the ground, Marion slammed her foot into his stomach. "You are under arrest, and you will face coven justice."

Ethan grabbed Marion's foot and pushed her off of him.

I opened the coffin's lid. I placed the chain in Pascaline's hands. "I'm sorry," I whispered.

There was a twitch as Pascaline's hand jerked away from the burning silver. Her eyes fluttered open. Her pupils were so large her irises disappeared. The whites of her eyes glowed in the darkness.

Pascaline's head rose from the pillow. Her eyes glittered as she pushed the chain away. Apparently, still half asleep, Pascaline reached up, but her hands didn't touch anything but stale black air.

"Oh, my god," Ethan whispered. "Pascaline!"

While Ethan's focus was on the rising vampire, I grabbed Marion's wrist. We slowly backed away. We stumbled over Gavin's dead body and crawled back into the light of the apartment.

In the Sanctum, Ethan screamed.

I looked back.

Pascaline's bare feet would have been silent except the bells jingling with every footstep. She backed Ethan into a wall. With ineffectual blows, he swiped and slapped at her. She ignored his struggles. She did not use a bleeding knife. Her fangs punctured his flesh as she took the blood which he had stolen.

I ran into the kitchenette. As expected, Ethan had stored several pints of blood in the fridge.

"What are you doing?" Marion screamed.

"Get Agata and Jakub! Derrik! I'm going to try to slow Pascaline! Hurry!"

Marion did so.

I was happy to see my most beloved coven sister awake, but wished Pascaline's visage wasn't terrifying. Her long auburn braids and black gown were sticky with Ethan's blood. My sneakers stuck to the spilled blood on the tile floor as I moved closer to the feeding vampire.

Pascaline lifted her eyes and set them on me but she did not take her lips off Ethan's wounds until his irises went milky and his flesh turned into a dry husk. She dropped him onto the floor. Unmoving. I admit I wanted to take a bite myself.

She turned toward me. Her wide-open eyes exposed her enlarged pupils. Her nostrils were sniffing around the room.

I held out a pint of blood. "Pascaline, my most beloved sister, it's me, Norma. I have a whole list of films for us to watch together. We finally got a Wonder Woman movie."

"There's an exhibit on Victorian Art at SAM and one about the Samurai. I hoped you would get to see it. Maybe we can take Derrik and Laurence."

Pascaline took a languid step, the bells on her ankle jingled.

I didn't move. Bloodlust engrossed Pascaline. Running, or even backing away, could cause my sister to react as if I were prey.

The elder took another step closer, and her expression was still unfamiliar.

"Callie?" Callie was the nickname only Loretta and I were allowed to use. I hoped it would help Pascaline return. I lifted the blood to Pascaline's eye level. Pascaline took the bag and drank it. She turned to me again, her teeth stained in red. Her eyes were strange and unknowing, alien, animal.

I gave her the second bag. I only had one more; hopefully, it was enough.

Pascaline punctured the second bag with her teeth and sucked out the blood; her eyes never left me. I saw when familiarity returned. "Callie?"

Pascaline licked out the bag. "Oh, *ma crevette*. Must you underdress for every occasion?"

"No one, but Marion knows you're up yet. And you're

still in your sleeping gown."

"Ah, so I am underdressed too." She licked her lips as more blood flowed into her mouth.

I glanced at Ethan, dead on the floor.

"Ethan chose his fate long ago. If it pains you, don't look at the corpse."

"You..."

She yawned. "I told him to go have a life before I went to sleep. He chose to remain on his own accord. Now, let's go to my apartment, and you can tell me all the gossip. How have you been?"

"I have a new friend. Carlos, he's a shade, but I know you'll just love him. Derrik loves him."

"But he's not a thrall?"

"No. Just a friend."

"Someday, Norma, your heart will open so wide it will feel like another death," she said sadly.

"Did you love Ethan like that?"

"Oh, you're such a romantic. I liked Ethan well enough, but I love Derrik and Laurence. How have they been?"

"Derrik's fine. He's upstairs. Hugo's injured his hip, so he's been worried."

"Hugo? How terrible. I must send a get well note. I'm still not quite awake; you won't let me forget?"

"I'll remind you." I handed Pascaline the last pint of blood. "Laurence bought a house up on Beacon Hill. I helped a little. Pretended to be his little sister because he scared his Realtor."

"You are his sister," Pascaline corrected me.

"I meant in the human way. I got to do movie makeup on him to hide his fangs."

"How droll!"

"It was fun." Arm in arm, we moved up the ramp to the coven. "You've missed so many movies. I've been keeping a list of the best ones," I said.

"And I can't wait to watch them with you, but I need to wake up a bit more, *ma chérie*," Pascaline replied.

Derrik and Agata met us on the stairs. Carlos and Marion stood behind them. And Jakub watched from somewhere. I felt his presence and did not doubt he was armed.

Marion's face had begun to swell where Ethan had got punches in. Derrik's eyes immediately ran over the burns on my hands, ripped sleeve, and bloody scalp.

"Oh, my daughter, you are awake." Agata stood straight and regal, but the slight tremble in her voice exposed that she was still weakened. Still, she was Agata.

Pascaline inclined her head. "Yes, Mother, I awoke a time ago. I must bathe and dress. I didn't wish Derrik to see me in this state. *Tu n'as rien, mon chér?*" (Are you okay, my dear?)

Derrik didn't answer her.

"Look at his eyes. He fears me, Mother."

With good reason, I thought.

"Have you eaten enough?" Agata asked.

"Norma and Ethan were there when I rose. Ethan gave me all. Norma's given me two, no three, pints already."

Derrik's eyes widened.

"From Ethan's fridge," I said. "Ethan's dead. Pascaline drank him dry, but I don't know if he's undead or what. I need to clean up the body. He staked Xiao and killed Irene."

"You have proof?" Agata asked.

"He confessed everything to Norma. I heard him and recorded his voice," Marion said. "He staked Xiao out of revenge, and from fear of retribution he drank from Pascaline. There is a silver chain in Pascaline's coffin. If we choose to test it, we will find his son's and Norma's burnt flesh on it. He was so messed up, probably from the bloodlust, he wanted to wake Pascaline and feed her Norma in revenge for the death of his son."

"I've heard enough," Derrik said, his voice full of anguish.

"So have I," Agata said. "Take a blood sample of whatever is left. We will hold an emergency meeting for coven justice. Derrik, stay with Pascaline. And Norma, get yourself cleaned up. You might be tempting Pascaline covered in so many wounds."

C ARLOS WATCHED FROM OVER AGATA'S shoulder.

I sensed he was furious I let myself be so ill-used, and he wasn't there to help me. Ethan was lucky that Pascaline just sucked him dry because Carlos wanted to rip him into tiny pieces. However, mindful of my reputation as well as the danger of a just awakened vampire, he didn't move to assist me. I was glad to have a friend and co-worker who understood vampires so well.

He wrote down: Lady Agata, if possible, after the investigation, might I have Ethan's eyes? My eyes are failing.

"Of course, dear," she replied. "Perhaps vampire eyes will remain fresher, longer. I'll harvest them for you and we can do the surgery this evening."

After Derrik escorted Pascaline up to her apartment, I returned to my office and collapsed onto my couch. Carlos locked the deadbolt and found the first aid kit. He carefully cleaned and bandaged my injuries as any fresh blood would be needed for the others.

"It took longer in real life than on movies to get Ethan to denounce himself," I said.

He didn't sign at me or write anything down. He merely finished his tasks. I waited.

Finally, he picked up a notebook and scrawled: In movies, the right to be silent is terrible for the plot.

Next time, don't be stupid. Let Marion take the knocks.

"I hope there isn't a next time."

He plopped down beside me on the couch. Me too. Working for the coven sucks.

L ATER THAT NIGHT, AFTER AGATA HAD fully awoken, Carlos was prepped for surgery. The operation was a success! I admit I wondered what other body parts we might find to help my friend exist even longer.

August 5, 2019

Chapter 24

7 PM

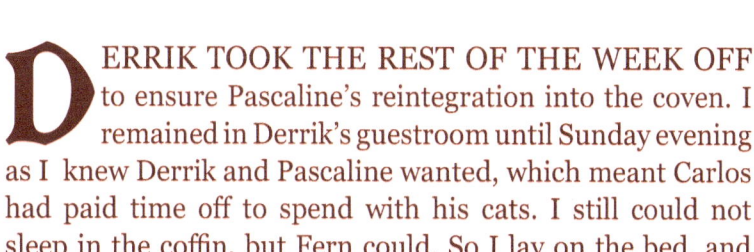

DERRIK TOOK THE REST OF THE WEEK OFF to ensure Pascaline's reintegration into the coven. I remained in Derrik's guestroom until Sunday evening as I knew Derrik and Pascaline wanted, which meant Carlos had paid time off to spend with his cats. I still could not sleep in the coffin, but Fern could. So I lay on the bed, and my eternally young body slept as soundly as I did at home. I ensured Hugo's comfort when Derrik was busy. Carlos and I even got Maria moved into the apartment down the hall.

Derrik and Pascaline leaned on each other for support as they had since Derrik's rebirth. Pascaline slipped into the French of her youth and even when she spoke in English her noble woman's accent seemed stronger than before. It wasn't a problem for Derrik or I as Pascaline taught us French long ago, but the young vampires who lived during the 1970s and '80s were not bilingual. Hugo and Carlos's Spanish was close enough that they understood much of what she said.

Xiao slowly recovered. He did not weep when Fern revealed to him privately that she was leaving him and becoming a vampire. Loretta and Charles were there to hold his hand. Their long bloodline ensured he was never alone. All he said was: "Fern has been unhappy for a long time. She'll make a good vampire. I wish her well."

Agata and Jakub announced Fern's entrance into the

program early, as Pascaline offered to guide her through the program and either she or Derrik would transform her into a vampire if that is what Fern ultimately decided.

However, as Fern feared, Bernie called her a power-hungry gold digger and asked if she wanted to end up like Ethan.

Hugo, Summer, and Kuma were more understanding and openly wished her well. Loretta's bloodline's thralls shunned her as did most of Charles's. When asked all that was ever said, is "We wish Fern well, but she is no longer one of us."

Fern, Ryan, and Pascaline came over to Derrik's and binge-watched several movies I suggested. We discussed the films. Pascaline asked questions about practical and computer effects. I regretted wishing for this very thing because it had come with Xiao's injuries and senseless deaths: Ethan, Irene, Gavin.

Of all the new technologies, Pascaline was most curious about the spread of cell phones. When she had gone to sleep in 2004, phones were not smart. Now everyone had them — except Derrik, who was always beside a computer and didn't see the point of squinting at a small screen when he had a large screen.

She interrogated us about smartphones. Since the non-charged cell phone was a common plot device in movies, Pascaline struggled with how many people with an immediate connection to the entire planet forgot to charge them.

And, I waited for Derrik and Pascaline to be alone with me before I asked Derrik. "Will it hurt you to see Laurence?"

"Of course not, but it was kind of you to ask," he said.

I texted Laurence: **Pascaline woke, but she doesn't have a cell yet, you'll need to call Derrik or me if you want to see her.**

Laurence: **Does she want to see me?**

Me: **Dude, call her**

Laurence: **She with you now?**
Me: **Yep**
Laurence: **Thanks.**

My phone rang in my hand. I passed it to Pascaline.

"How did you know he'd call so quick?" Derrik asked.

"I did a job for him. He kept asking about her."

"Too bad we can't get him to reside in the coven like a normal vampire," Derrik said. I thought it might start a complaint, but he didn't criticize Capitol Hill.

Pascaline fell into French as she tried to make a date. Laurence's Italian allowed him to understand most of the words, but like other vampires who just arose from a long sleep, Pascaline grew confused. Eventually, I took the phone back.

"Laurence, Saturday won't work. There's a coven funeral for Ethan."

"Whose Ethan?" he asked.

"A vampire who died," I said.

"Does Pascaline need me there?"

I glanced at Derrik and mouthed "funeral."

He shook his head.

"No. Derrik and I'll be there for her."

"She's in love with him? This Ethan?" Laurence spit out the name Ethan as if it was a curse. He was used to sharing her with Derrik, but he didn't hide his jealousy at new people.

"Not like she loves you and Derrik, but it was upsetting. Look, either hookup with my sister or not."

"It's not a hookup. It never is," he said.

I fought rolling my eyes. I didn't care what they called their relationship. Back when the men were young vampires, there weren't words for such a romance — or all the words were negative. All that mattered were the three were content enough.

"Does Pascaline have plans on Tuesday?" he asked.

"He will pick you up on Tuesday night. You're going

for a walk in the Arboretum."

"So I'm taking her to the Arboretum?" Laurence asked.

"Yeah. She'll like it and needs a restful date — or whatever old vampires are calling it nowadays. Plus, if she needs to hunt..."

"I understand."

"Oh, and since I have you on the phone, there's a new exhibit over at SAM. I thought once Pascaline's completely back on her feet, the four of us could go. I didn't ask him yet, but maybe Derrik's Secondborn too. He needs to get out of the coven and chill."

His tone said: *I'd love hanging out with you and Pascaline, but I really don't want to hang out with a bunch of freaking Dracula-wannabe-vampires.* He said, "I guess I'm okay with that as long as Derrik's okay with it. Who's his Secondborn again?"

Good enough.

ON FRIDAY NIGHT, THE THRALLS PREPARED Ethan's ashes. Saturday night was a somber funeral which Agata led.

I wish I could say this was the first vampire funeral I have attended, but it is not. Ethan was not considered a coven member or even Pascaline's Secondborn, but a rogue vampire of the coven's acquaintance. The rest was hushed up because that was how the coven rolled.

Derrik and I sat on either side of Pascaline and held her hand as she watched in quiet mourning. For her prostrations, she did not love Ethan, bloody tears rolled down her cheeks, and she sobbed openly. I knew my coven sister too well. There was plenty of room for love in her vampire's heart. Watching my sister grieve, I thought of Derrik's claim that vampires loved all of their creations. Maybe he was right.

Beside Derrik, Ryan had a steady supply of

handkerchiefs and even a pint of blood.

On the other side of me sat Alice and her husband. Behind us sat not only the entirety of the Paper Flower Consortium, most of the Bellevue coven. Others came from Spokane and Vancouver.

They came to support Pascaline in her grief.

FTER BREAKFAST THE NEXT SUNSET, I drove my van north from Georgetown, through SoDo, the international district, downtown, and east to Capitol Hill. Even with Derrik and Pascaline, I did not feel the pulse of life in Georgetown. I never did. In Capitol Hill, I found myself happy and relaxed again.

The condo was how I left it. Everything in its place. The bright yellow walls lightened my spirit as they always did. Fridge empty. But that didn't matter in this neighborhood. Music leeched through the walls from the club below. I felt the beat of the city, its pulse as rich as any human heart.

I opened the west-facing window. I looked down the hill beyond downtown's skyscrapers toward Elliot Bay, reflecting the boats, the buildings, hiding its secrets. I inhaled the smell of algae as the breeze came from the west.

The homeless slept in the urine-soaked alleyways or panhandled. Hipsters laughed as they moved in and out of the establishments. A woman walked her two dogs which growled at the sky, sensing my inhumanity. A man ducked behind a dumpster and took a piss against the old brick and cobbled stones. Three laughing drunk women stumbled on too-high heels.

Even on a Sunday, I loved Capitol Hill.

I texted Carlos: I'm back at work tomorrow if you're ready. If not, let me know when you want to come back on.

Carlos: Good. Pick me up at the station. I'm so bored. The cats aren't learning cat tricks, but they're training me.

He sent a video. Carlos coaxed his cat, Mittens, to jump through a hoop. Mittens sat purring until he gave up and handed him the treat.

Me: **LOL. Mittens is a genius!**

Below, one of the women leaned on the wall and adjusted her shoe. I probably could take out all three women, but that wouldn't be much of a hunt. I wanted fresh blood. Young blood.

Vampire-friendly bars often looked the other way when I came into work, but I didn't want to press my luck when I was there socially. I padded my chest and hips. I did my make-up and hairstyle carefully, adding streaks of red in the dark curls and contouring my cheeks to look older. I slipped on a light weight red sheath with a lacing at the neckline.

I passed the open arcade with its flashing lights, restaurants, and clubs until I entered the one I wanted.

Then I found my favorite type of victim: a man, twenty-one, looking for a good time with a vampire and not much else. He just wanted a memory and to see if it was real. He had no interest in being a thrall. He didn't even know of such things. If I let him live, he wouldn't try to find me afterwards.

I took him behind the bar to the dark private room in the back. It was clumsy on his part, but his blood was sweet.

I dabbed a little Neosporin on his wound so the cut would heal cleanly. He asked for my number.

Since most needed calories after a donation, I asked if he wanted another drink, took him back into the bar and bought him a beer, hamburger, and fries.

I let him remember a fun moment and nothing more. He wouldn't even remember the blood, just that he had a good time with a vampire chick. Or maybe a goth chick who pretended to be a vampire.

Then I left.

It was all I could do while remaining within the boundaries of the law. Listening to snippets of music, I walked along Broadway, seeking a second victim. Maybe a woman this time.

One day Derrik would go into torpor. One day, I would. Pascaline slept in the so-called safety of the coven, and was still in danger. The seas would rise. Animals would become extinct.

It was a different world and changing every day.

Immortality was terrifying.

"BLOODY" SAVORY SHORTBREAD

Goat Cheese Filling

8 oz Goat Cheese	1/4 cup Cream
1 teaspoon Basil	Dash of Black Pepper

Mix all ingredients in bowl

Sun Dried Tomato Jam aka the blood

One 8-ounce jar sun-dried tomatoes packed in oil

2 tablespoons sugar	1/4 cup red wine vinegar
1 cup water	Salt and Pepper to taste

Place a medium saucepan over medium heat. Drain and chopped sun dried tomatoes reserve oil. Add sun-dried tomatoes, two tablespoons of reserved oil and onion to pan. Stir and cook until onions are soft and begin to brown. 5 to 7 minutes. Add the sugar, vinegar, water. Bring to a boil, reduce the heat, and simmer, covered, for 30 minutes. Remove the cover and continue simmering until most of the liquid is reduced and the mixture is the consistency of jam, about 5 - 10 more minutes. Remove from the heat and set aside. Cool.
Add Salt and Pepper to taste.

Short bread Crackers

1 1/4 cups whole wheat flour	1 tablespoon sugar
1/2 teaspoon Kosher salt	4 tablespoons unsalted butter
1/3 cup water	1 teaspoon of paprika

Preheat the oven to 400 F. Line baking sheets with parchment paper. Mix flour, sugar, salt, and paprika. Add butter and blend until butter is fully incorporated. (A food processor or heavy mixer makes this easier) Add water and blend until smooth dough forms. Divide it into 4 equal-size pieces. Lightly flour your work surface and roll a dough pieces into a large rectangle. Roll dough until it is 1/8 of an inch. Using a knife or cookie cutters cut in 1" squares
Bake crackers on parchment-lined baking sheet until lightly browned, about 10 minutes. When cool, pipe or spread filling on cracker. Top with tomato jam and second cracker

ABOUT THE AUTHOR

MUCH TO HER CHAGRIN, ELIZABETH Guizzetti discovered she was not a cyborg and growing up to be an otter would be impractical, so began writing stories at age twelve. Three decades later, Guizzetti is an illustrator and author best known for her demon-poodle based comedy, *Out for Souls & Cookies.* She is also the creator of *For the Love of Pancakes*, *Faminelands* and *Lure* and collaborated with authors on several projects including *A is for Apex* and *The Prince of Artemis V*.

To explore a different aspect of her creativity, she writes science fiction and fantasy. Her debut novel, *Other Systems*, was a 2015 Finalist for the Canopus Award for excellence in Interstellar Fiction. Her short work has appeared in anthologies such as *Wee Folk and The Wise* and *Beyond the Hedge*. Other credits include: *Immortal House, The Grove Chronicles of the Martlet*, and *The Light Side of the Moon.*

Guizzetti lives in Seattle with her husband and dogs. When not writing or illustrating, she loves hiking and birdwatching.

To find out more about her work follow her on
Instagram: @elizabeth_guizzetti
Facebook: /Elizabeth.Guizzetti.Author
Twitter @E_Guizzetti
Web: https://www.elizabethguizzetti.com

PAPER FLOWER CONSORTIUM BOOKS:

Norma's Cleaning Services Mysteries

Death Pulls a Stake Out, 2018
Death Hears a Siren, 2019
Death Sticks a Pixie, 2019

Elder's of the Paper Flower Consortium

Honor Among Vampires, 2019 (Agata)
Chivalry Among Vampires, 2020 (Jakub)
And more stories to come!

Immortal House, 2018 (Laurence's Story)

Vampires of the Paper Flower Consortium Podcast

is found on most podcatchers!

OTHER PROJECTS

Other Systems
The Light Side of the Moon
The Grove

COMICS

For Blood, Bones, & Biscuits
Faminelands
Lure
Out for Souls and Cookies
The Prince of Artemis V (Illustrator)
A is for Apex (Illustrator)